KING ALFRED'S COLLEGE
WINCHESTER
Library: 01962 827306

To be returned on or before the day
marked below, subject to recall

Sound, Speech, and Music

SOUND,

SPEECH,

AND MUSIC

David Burrows

The University of Massachusetts Press

Amherst

Copyright © 1990 by
The University of Massachusetts Press
All rights reserved
Printed in the United States of America
LC 89–4947
ISBN 0–87023–685–7
Designed by Barbara Werden
Set in Linotron Trump Medieval
at Keystone Typesetting, Inc.

Library of Congress Cataloging-in-Publication Data
Burrows, David L.
  Sound, speech, and music / David Burrows.
    p. cm.
  Includes index.
  ISBN 0–87023–685–7 (alk. paper)
  1. Music—Philosophy and aesthetics. 2. Sound. 3. Speech.
I. Title.
ML3845.B837 1990
780'.1—dc20   89–4947
                            CIP
                            MN

British Library Cataloguing in Publication
data are available.

Contents

Acknowledgments

B E L O W   I S   A partial list of readers of earlier versions of some of the material in this book who have reacted with criticism and encouragement, both of them useful, both of them received with gratitude: Rita Aiello, Jeannette H. Alimonda, Lia Rejane Mendes Barcellos, Elaine Bearer, Stanley Boorman, Salwa El-Shawan, Steven Feld, Mark Germer, Gabriela Ilnitchi, Jan LaRue, Linda Laurent, Siegmund Levarie, Tilman Seebass, Kay Kaufman Shelemay, Douglas Sobers, Maynard Solomon, Anthony Storr, Fiorenza Weinapple; the participants in the "Forskningsseminar I, Musikkestetikk" held at the University of Oslo in November 1987, especially its organizers Even Ruud and Ståle Wikshåland; and the members of the music therapists' retreat at Phoenicia, in particular Helen Bonny, Barbara Hesser, and Carolyn Kenny (especially for her work on the "field of play"). I owe a special debt to Benjamin Boretz, whose response some years ago to an early version of Chapter 1 (a tactful version of "so what?") set me in motion on the path that has led to this book. Special thanks to Christopher Collins, who has twice been my partner in team-taught "words and music" courses at New York University; my understanding of the subjects addressed in this book has grown in measure as he has added to it and challenged it.

Certain parts of the book have already appeared in different form: Chapter 1 as "On Hearing Things" in *Musical Quarterly* 66, no. 2 (1980); Chapter 3 as "Sound and the Emergence of Mind" in *Journal of Social and Biological Structures* 8 (1985); Chapter 4 as "Singing and Saying" in *Journal of Musicology* 7 (Summer 1989), © 1989 by the Regents of the University of California; Chapter 6 as "How Well Does Music Survive Our Representations Of It?" in *Studia Musicologica Norvegica* 14 (1988); Chapter 7 as "Instrumentalities" in *Journal of Musicology* 5, no. 1 (Winter 1987), © 1987 by the Regents of the University of California; and an outline of the central argument as "Speaking and Singing" in *Perspectives of New Music* 17, no. 2 (1979).

Sound, Speech, and Music

Introduction

THREE FIELDS OF

HUMAN ACTION

F O R   M O S T   P E O P L E most of the time, sound is one
of the unconsidered ubiquities, as transparent to scrutiny as the air
that carries it. To the extent it gets reasoned consideration at all it
is as a means to such ends as talk or music—as a means, in other
words, to the ends first of communication and second of entertain-
ment. Beyond the foreground made up of these organized activities
lies the free-form, often purposeless jumble of the sounds of foot-
steps in gravel, bird song, passing trucks, the wind—an incessant
background to our lives from which details often emerge that play
an important part in orientation.

This book sets out to consider what influence the specific
character of the means, in the case of sound, may have had on the
form taken by its ends of communication in man; and what the
consequences for man's nature may have been of adapting to

sound's unique potential for communication. My thesis is that the distinctiveness of human beings as a species—in particular their capacity for free-wheeling and wide-ranging thought—is to a great extent an outgrowth of the distinctiveness of the way they use sound, itself distinctive in a number of ways among the senses.

Though the thesis is broad, the reader will quickly pick up a tilt toward musical issues and values in its presentation, a tilt that is unavoidable since the author comes to the subject with the training and preoccupations of a musician. In its earliest stages, in fact, the project that has produced this book was a quest for an ontology of music, but the roots of music in sound are the roots of speech as well, and so the enterprise opened out to include the ontology of speech and of thought generally.

Instead of basing the search in one of the traditional academic disciplines, I have chosen to refer my phenomenology of sound, speech, thought, and music to a scheme (for which I claim no particular originality) that characterizes the individual, living human body as a center with a strong instinctual tendency to treat everything else in the cosmos as peripheral to it—though at times it may choose to assign other entities priority over itself. Life is seen here as a radiation around a center. The further it radiates— the more territory it controls—the more secure it feels (but the center/periphery scheme applies not only to relations between the body and its surroundings; it organizes the interior world of the body itself as well). This means that the centripetal/centrifugal coordinate of action, governing motion toward and away from the center, is fundamental, and the self is defined whenever the force of its centrifugally radiating energies encounters the resistance of the "other." The self is the other than other.

The scheme is no purely spatial one, for the spatial center

4

is ultimately the focus of all value as well (and value is dispersed around the center in a pattern with no direct relation to distance from the center).

People may move in a body, act as a body: social life is the coordination of overlapping individual center/periphery schemes in overlapping clusters such as family and village and guild, themselves each governed by the same scheme. These superbodies are at once far more powerful and far more clumsily articulated than the individual ones making them up.

On both its individual and social levels, the center/periphery scheme is projected in three basic fields with their associated topologies, arranged below in order of decreasing structural rigidity. Topologies are here taken to be the configurations that define the action possible in some field.

Field 1 is physical space, the space taken up by the body and through which the body moves, the space surveyed by the senses, with vision bearing the heaviest responsibility among them. In this field the center is always identified with the physical body. It takes precedence over the other fields to the extent that the physical survival of the self is at issue.

The basic coordinates of the topology governing Field 1 are set by the localization of the body in the lateral dimension of physical space, which brings with it a unidirectional dynamic to the vertical dimension by pulling the body and the physical objects it deals with tight to ground level. Because the body is mobile, the specific content of up and down and of near and far is subject to continuous change through which the topological coordinates themselves remain constant.

Movement makes degrees of solidity a central consideration in this field, because the moving body needs solidity to push

5

off from but experiences varying degrees of difficulty in passing through it. Further categories of the topology of Field 1 include: inside/outside the body, along with the degrees of withinness and withoutness, and the threshold between them; separation/connection and its degrees: separation/connection between bodies, between the body and things, between and among things.

Field 2 is the invisible and intangible space where thought takes place—the Stoic *pneuma*, Lucretius's "mind-stuff," the Cartesian *res cogitans*. If Field 1 is the world inhabited by the body, Field 2 lays out the options open to the mind. This mental space takes on where the senses, rooted to the here and now, leave off—in fact, it can be thought of as an alternative to being stuck fast in Field 1, as a way to gain perspective on the here and now in order to establish increased control over it. Though action in this field takes place inside the body and, like all action, in the now, yet by means of such action the here and now is opened out to include past, future, elsewhere: enter memory, conjecture, plans, and expectations. Because the entities in play in this field are not sensory data, they can ultimately be validated only by social consensus, by an agreement among the community of their users to act as though they had an ontological status equivalent to that of objects in Field 1. The free-wheeling style of action in Field 2 earns its Darwinian keep when its constructions are translated into enduring physical and social terms: the artifacts, the institutions, the works of humans. From pliers to codes of law these function as a protective zone interpolated between individuals and groups and their "other."

Attention is the body's outrider in Field 1, attending to its physical orientation; in Field 2 it becomes the center and weaves patterns of thought by moving from subject to subject (concepts, images) and connecting them as a shuttle might, in the process creating the field that holds them—for Field 2 is no a priori receptacle waiting to receive action, as is Field 1, but is itself a function of action. Only its potential contents (an inventory of concepts and images) and the rules for realizing it are there in advance.

Because past, future, elsewhere—the extensions of Field 1 that are distinctive of Field 2—are immaterial and synthetic categories brought into being by action, the constraints on action in this field are synthetic too, translations into new, more abstract terms of the resistance and continuity that support action in Field 1. They are far looser than those of Field 1: a large distance between two points in physical space is no impediment to their confrontation here; everything in the inventory is accessible at any time; here there is no asymmetrical gravitational field tending to pull all objects up against something corresponding to the earth's surface.

But constraints there are. The requirement of intelligibility imposes on speech the procedural constraint of pairing noun phrase and verb phrase, labeling a provisional center for attention and attributing a defining periphery to it. On another level there is the constraint on discourse of plausibility, of correspondence to the way things might actually be, and this has an interpersonal dimension, the acceptability of a speech act to an interlocutor. Correspondence has many focal lengths, many degrees of attention to the way things are (or supposedly were, or may be some day), running, for example, from that of the police blotter to that of a grand-unified-field theory, but some degree of detachment and play in the relationship between representation and object is characteristic of all action in Field 2. Other constraints include logic and clarity: the more detached a discourse the greater tends to be the role in it of considerations of good design. Correspondence can, of course, be suspended altogether, in the interests, perhaps, of art, or treachery, or compassion.

The immaterial, synthetic nature of its contents and topology and the free play in the relationship between its representations and their objects give to Field 2 a dangerous freedom: so much to control, so much to go wrong. Field 2 is the domain of reason—and of madness and violence.

Field 3   Body, then mind; finally, the field of the spirit—if "spirit" can be understood in a not primarily theological way as referring to the sense of self as diffused through the full range of awareness. For this is the field whose center, in the formulation of medieval mystics, "is everywhere and its periphery nowhere." Freud wrote of the "oceanic feeling"; a latter-day image for it is the hologram. Territoriality is clearly no issue here, for there is no particularity in Field 3, no this and that; the dualities of self and other and near and far survive here in attenuated form, if at all. Action tends to be suspended or to assume cyclic, self-enfolded forms. This is the field of neonates and mystics, approximated in varying degrees by the rest of the population through their participation in music and the other arts or through meditation and ritual. Though involvement in Field 3 can be solipsistic, it can also suffuse a group of musical performers, for example, or ritual celebrants.

In Field 1 the view is the view from here; in Field 2, the view from anywhere you can name or imagine; in Field 3 the view from everywhere, of an undifferentiated everywhere. Fields 2 and 3 can be thought of as ways to transcend the limits of bodily existence in Field 1, and Field 3 also offers relief from the pressures of living in Field 2. None of them is completely discrete and independent of the others. Each of them can be entered into with varying degrees of intensity and commitment, and it is normal to operate simultaneously in Fields 1 and 2, or in 1 and 3, or in all three at once, cutting back and forth and interweaving material from them all.

H O W   D O E S   sound figure in any of this? My thesis is that sound has played a massively liberating role in human evolution, the key role in the development of what is most distinctive about humans as a species; that sound was indispensable to the elaboration of Field 2 and to the parallel opening up of Field 3. First among human distinctions comes thought. No other organism approaches our capacity to perform shareable but skin-in manipulations that are not only predominantly about what lies outside the organism but are also disengaged from the immediate domain of the senses in the instant and that range far over past and future and elsewhere. Chief vehicle of thought is speech, and of speech, sound, and I will argue that sound is far more to speech than a passive conveyance. I suggest rather that human thought has evolved its expansiveness and freedom in large part through exploiting the unique capacity of vocal sound for rapidity of articulation in detachment from the world of enduring spatial objects.

If this is so, then it is surprising that sound, in all its particularity, has no more solid a place in our picture of the human adaptive strategy than it does. But solidity is not a characteristic of the auditory experience, as it is of the visual; perhaps the difficulty lies right here. Though thinking is movement, it is movement inspired by an ideal and a goal of eventual fixity; though it may be carried, and shaped, and furthered by vocal sound, it aspires to vision, to the kind of control over clear and stable configurations that seeing can give us. Inquisitiveness is a matter of wanting to get the picture—the picture of the human adaptive strategy, for example—and to put the inquirer in that picture. Never visible, never still, sound is by its nature radically resistant to direct scrutiny and to insertion into any static explanatory scheme—unless it is first given a visual representation such as a written script, a graph, or a musical score, and with sound such representation is to an exceptional degree misrepresentation (this point is elaborated in Chapter 6).

Processes of all kinds resist the sort of picturing that thought aims at, and this applies not only to sound but also to the process of thinking itself, whose great virtue lies in its free-flowing and wide-ranging quality: thought is a sort of paradoxical listening for a fixed and sharply focused vision of the world. No such vision of thought would be true to its dynamic nature. Thought eludes thought, as sound does.

If neither sound nor thought submits easily to formulation, then it is no surprise that thinkers on human nature have not taken the further step of dwelling on their similarities, or the yet-further step of speculating that these similarities might not be coincidental but rather point to an ancient interdependency between them, the elaboration of thought through the agency of sound. That conjectural interdependency is the subject of the present book.

THE FOCAL point of my argument is Chapter 3, dealing with speech. Insofar as it is a physical action in which one person's vocal apparatus affects the hearing of others here and now, speaking takes place in Field 1. But unlike most actions, spoken utterances typically have their justification in their connection with something that isn't there, available to the senses of speaker and listener at the time of the action. In this they are distinct not just from such actions as peeling and eating an orange but from other specifically communicative acts as well, such as waving or calling. Their import may have no obvious connection of any kind with the place and the moment the action occurs. Speech gives a kind of presence to things not physically present, speakers and listeners assuming an as-if orientation toward situations that don't in physical fact obtain. This potential for radical disengagement from the immediate is the feature that most clearly differentiates speech from the communicative acts of other species, more than any other the feature that was responsible for its evolutionary emergence and success and responsible ultimately for making humans, the only talking animals, the dominant presence on the planet.

Radical disengagement opened the way for the vast expansion of Field 2. I will argue that all this resulted from the exploitation in speech of sound's relative disengagement from the topology of Field 1: this feature of sound may be an important piece of the puzzle that is the emergence of the human mind. Sound could have its effect once we evolved the articulatory and cognitive apparatus for exploiting the possibility of using a nonlikeness, in the form of a vocal signal, as a form of representation.

Chapter 1 prepares the way for this with a general discussion of the nature of sound. Sound is not here treated as an acoustician or a physiologist or a psychologist would treat it. Rather it is engaged at the level of and in the language of everyday experience, for its broad contribution to orientation. Discussion proceeds by means of a running comparison of sound with sight, the other principal sense for picking up information at a distance, for the way they deal with a number of issues that are crucial to orientation, such as the relationship of the signal to its source, its relationship to the receiver, questions of distance and direction and temporality. Sound is far more lightly attached to Field 1 than is sight, and its independence of the topography of Field 1 is suggestive of that of Field 2.

In Chapter 2 the voice is discussed as the most intimate and powerful human exploitation of the potential in sound, a means of displaying mood and attitude and a way of bonding separate individuals and negotiating their mutual interests. A model is proposed for explaining the expressive workings of the voice whose theme is the interaction of force with resistance. It draws a parallel between the confrontation of breath with larynx that results in the sound of the voice, and that of the self with its world: according to this model, the force with which air is exhaled from the lungs and the resistance it meets from the vocal folds mime the resistance offered by the world to the centrifugal energies of the self, with the result that the sound of the voice, its timbre and volume, can be read as an index of the vocalizer's state of mind. It is the share of the world in this confrontation that is enormously expanded and differentiated when lips, teeth, and tongue further resist and articulate the stream of sound from the larynx to produce the phonemes of speech.

The process whereby an organism achieves and maintains its sense of identity in relation to its world is far more complex—and potentially more treacherous—for a speaker than it is for an inarticulate animal, in whose sense of self the immediate input of the senses plays a relatively greater role. If speech is a displacement of the mutual awareness of speaker and listener from Field 1, the here and now surveyed by the senses, and into the metasensory domain of Field 2, then the speaking self is defined by its relationship to shifting possibilities outside the actuality of the moment, possibilities at best indirectly verifiable. This means that a corresponding quality of contingency and provisionality must characterize that range of identity which is at the focus of speech and speech-related thought. Music is seen in Chapter 4 as one of a range of activities that help compensate for this debilitation of identity by moving the participant's orientation toward that of Field 3. The centripetal energies of music are contrasted with the centrifugal thrust of speech: the mechanism and strategies distinctive of speech and song are deployed in a contrastive ordering in which the traits associated with song are linked to more primitive and central aspects of both vocalizer and listener, in evolutionary, developmental, spatial, and temporal terms. The concept of "protosemiosis" is brought in to describe the nonsymbolic, nonreferential level of communication that predominates in music.

Chapter 5 takes up what happens when speech and music converge in song. Physical survival is more closely dependent on speech than it is on music, and so it seems that allowing music to win out in a confrontation between the two amounts to succumbing to a mini-death wish—yet this is just what happens in most vocal music. The explanation for this outcome offered here hinges in part on the homeostatic function claimed for music in the previous chapter—there are times when it is healthy to die to the dominant adaptive modality—and in part on the argument that attention, given a real choice, will take the path of lesser resistance. Music offers less resistance than speech does, principally because its near lack of a semantic component means that taking it in involves one cognitive operation less than does understanding speech.

Song is one of two activities involving a close relationship between words and music. Words may tend to get upstaged when they are set to music in song, but the two have a completely different relationship when music is put into words, when words are the medium for a descriptive, or analytical, or critical account of music. In such cases the initiative lies with the words. Chapter 6 takes on the larger question of music and its representations, setting a discussion of verbal representations of music in the context of graphic and gestural instances (scores, for example, and the conductor's performance). I propose that the gap between the positions occupied by object and representation along the continuums diffuseness/concentration and flow/fixity tends to be especially wide in the case of music, and this gap is made the occasion for reflections about the nature of music and the nature of representation generally.

The themes of fixity as opposed to flow and diffuseness as opposed to concentration that are central to the discussion of representations in Chapter 6 surface in a different musical setting in the last chapter, Chapter 7. Because they are fixed and concentrated physical objects, instruments are a musical entry in Field 1, the world of everyday things, and they are a means of getting our hands on the flowing diffuseness of music in somewhat the way we close with mechanical problems with the help of such nonmusical instruments as hammers and steam irons. Musical instruments may fulfill such nonmusical roles as transitional object, or mask, but in at least one respect they have a purely musical advantage over the voice, most natural of musical means: because of the degree to which they depersonalize the performer they put fewer distractions in the way of the listener's approach to Field 3.

Chapter One

————————

SOUND

————————
————
——

IMAGINE A BELL ringing, a series of sharp explo-
sions followed by tremulous dyings-away. The ringing is continuously making way for itself, each moment is new. Unlike the cool
constancy of the visual image of the bell, there to be seen whenever
I choose to look and as long as there is light, so that it seems to be
waiting on my pleasure, the ringing comes and goes independently
of my wish to take it in. I must adapt to it. I respond to its unre-
liability with a feeling of empathy. The ringing is a sign of something out there, outside my own delimited and contingent being,
with some of the same surge and flux I know in myself. I am not
alone in being under way, growing and fading, pausing, then starting up again, and I feel confirmed.

The ringing reaches me with the intimacy of a touch, and
this intensifies the feeling of self-confirmation. To see the bell I

must turn toward it and focus on it, reach out myself and touch it with my attention; and nothing would be easier than to withdraw my touch by shutting my eyes or looking away. The sound, like the touch of a hand moved by a will other than my own, is not so easily ignored: I cannot shut nonexistent earlids. Sight draws me out, sound finds me here. And sound goes beyond touch, which respects the perimeter of my skin, and beyond its degree of intimacy in seeming to be going on within me as much as around me.

Looking at the bell locates it off over there, and me back here. But if I shut my eyes, shutting out the extension of things in space, the ringing goes on as before. It floats free, filling in around me; I can attach it to the physical fact of the bell over there if I choose, but nothing about the ringing compels me to. The notion I get from it of the direction and distance from me of its source is vague compared to what looking at the bell would provide; still less is ringing bell-shaped: if I can derive the size and shape of the bell from its ringing it is because I have heard bells before while I watched them ring. The bell is off over there; the ringing is here, and there, and all around, within me and without. While I listen the whole notion of separateness and distance fades as a perceptual issue.

Sound is one of the two major ways we are aware of anything at all at a distance. Light and air connect us across the spaces that separate us, and their states change in detectable ways in response to our movements. By reading the changes as, for example, the sight of a figure running, or perhaps the sound of whistling or hallooing, we can stay tenuously connected with each other while apart. Our communities stretch and contract ceaselessly as the individuals that make them up stream and flow through the biofilm, foraging, building, exchanging. We wave and shout and point across the gaps between us because the more we can load into the variabilities of light and air of the past and future and elsewhere, of memory and planning, the more richly connected we will be. Extending our control over these variabilities to, above all, speech and writing is the basis of our distended elastic togetherness in large communities.

H E A R I N G I S the dark first-born sibling of sight. Indifferent to the presence or absence of light and relatively indifferent too to the kinds of distinctions light helps us to make, it is already formed in the dark world of gestation before we emerge into the illuminated one: we are all of us listeners before we are viewers. An unborn child may startle in the womb at the sound of a door slamming shut. The rich warm cacophony of the womb has been recorded: the mother's heartbeat and breathing are among the earliest indications babies have of the existence of a world beyond their own skin.

And sound collaborates with touch to ease the transition from the warm, stable world of the womb to the open randomness of the outside; for example, newborn infants kept in a nursery where a recording of the sound of a heart beating is played are more contented than those swaddled in silence.

But once children have emerged and grown, nothing is more basic to them than their mobile localization in Field 1—their need to approach things, get out of their way, or pick their way past them—and of all the senses, seeing gives them the most help with all this. All questions of how far away things are, of how distant from each other, and of how large they are and in what direction they are moving and how fast are best answered by looking. Vision sorts things out in space, putting them in their places in relation to each other and to us, and so for most purposes we must give it first place. Far more often we look around because of something we have heard than we listen because of something we have seen.

A sound can certainly give its hearers some idea of the location of its source. But the impression is weaker by far than the one provided by sight, whose reliability about direction, for example—to take one of the basic parameters of Field 1—has to do with the behavior of light. Light can always be trusted to reach the eye by a straight path that can be traced back to its source. This can be a limitation when the straight line between object and viewer is obstructed. In such cases sound can be a help, as long as precise information about the direction in which the object lies isn't essential, because instead of traveling in straight lines it moves in shock waves that balloon out invisibly around some source of disturbance, filling in around objects in its path as does its carrier, the air. Air is all around us and consequently sound is too, coming at the hearer from all sides, though the stimulus is usually stronger coming from the direction of the source. There is no facing away from a sound. When the volunteers of the fire company need to assemble, they blow a siren; they don't hang out a sign.

Looking out a window at night from a lighted room we see an image of the contents of the room behind us, reflected in the glass and superimposed on the scene outside. Such palimpsests are a chance and unimportant part of visual experience, but they are the norm for hearing. Sounds flow over and through each other and jut up in one another's midst in ways that bear no resemblance to the ways their sources relate in space. For a listener, the topology of Field 1, in which clearly defined objects and spaces are seen arranged discretely outside each other—whether next to, behind, or on top of each other, closer to or farther off—shades over into one in which different and shifting densities, textures, and intensities of activity coexist in varying degrees of interpenetration. Sound always deals in non-Euclidean geometry.

Because sound breaks with the topology of Field 1, so must the uses people make of it, including the sound of the voice and the articulations of the voice into speech and song. It follows that the topology of Field 1 fails as a model for understanding these activities and the processes of thought associated with them. This book proposes two alternate models, Fields 2 and 3, to account for both the freedom and the constraints special to verbal and musical thinking.

S O U N D I S vague enough about location but tells us nothing at all about the finer details of spatial disposition we call appearance. Touch is the other sense, besides sight, that has directly to do with the disposition of things in space and the details of the way they take up room. In the case of seeing, light does a measure of our groping for us, at a distance: it is resisted by the contours and textures of things, much as hands would be, and we read its deflections and qualifications as their appearance. Echolocation, the analogous use of self-generated sound for navigational purposes by bats and some other animals, is not one of the central human skills. Not even bats can read the contours of objects in the sounds the objects themselves produce; in both literal and figurative senses, such sounds give us rumors—mysterious or frightening ones sometimes—not facts.

If a sound is to lead us back to the spatial world we must interpret it. Often this is guesswork. In cases where we are sure that such and such a sound was made by a dropped garbage pail or by a plucked guitar string, it is knowledge derived from earlier experience of guitars and garbage pails and the sounds they produce.

Besides, most sounds are made by only a part of what sight would identify as their sources. The visible world is a world of surfaces, because light mostly comes from outside and elsewhere and plays off those surfaces (light bulbs and phosphorescent deep-sea creatures that generate their own visual appearance belong to the exceptions), leaving viewers to deduce for themselves the volume and make-up of what lies beneath. As with the human voice, sound often issues from a location hidden within the source, a point to be taken up again in Chapter 7. It is not the whole singer that is vibrating, yet the whole singer may be of spatial interest. In all of this there is all too much room for slippage and deception. If "seeing is believing," then hearing is in fact often a matter of guessing and hoping. People speak of the light—but not of the sound—of reason.

Under some circumstances we enjoy the suffusiveness of sound as a quality in itself, detached from the practical advantages or disadvantages that go with it. It would take radical surgery to separate the visual image of singers, while we are watching them perform, from their places on the stage. The music they sing, on the other hand, while it clearly starts out from the stage, expands outward from there in every direction.

Sound is literally disembodiment, an emanation from the bodies producing it that leaves their materiality and concentrated localization behind. The singers themselves have the sensation of expanding, in attenuated form, into surrounding space and filling it; and when their listeners close their eyes, the whole auditorium becomes their music. What expands outward from them in every direction presses in on the audience from all sides, neutralizing the normally charged issue of here and there.

All this takes place without any overt activity on the part

of the listeners. Looking is an outwardly active process, involving as it does active movements of the eyes, head, trunk, and body to achieve favorable orientation and focus. The field of vision is a swiveling cone of receptivity, like a reverse-flow searchlight with which we scan our surroundings. But we stop to listen: inwardly, listening may be just as active as looking, but outwardly we will often arrest movement and wait for the sound to come clear. Seeing is like touching, hearing like being touched; except that the touch of sound does not stop at the skin. It seems to reach inside and to attenuate, along with the distinction in Field 1 between here and there, the biologically still more basic one between within and without. In this way sound can ease some of the tension that goes with the duality of the organic condition.

W I T H A large area of overlap, sight and sound favor two different fundamental aspects of the world. At the same time that the viewer in each of us is stepping back from the world and sorting its contents out into discrete entities, the listener in each of us is merging and moving along with a range of its activity. We see the world as a noun and hear it as a verb. For vision, things have their places: this is the world in its aspect of fixity and reliability. As stated earlier, sound is comparatively weak in the issues of practical geometry that are basic to Field 1. The scuffling that sounds as though it is coming from the fire escape is actually taking place in the hallway. What sounds like a creaking shoe proves to be a creaking shutter. Instead, sound favors the world as process. As a general rule, visual data are informative by virtue of taking up the visual field unevenly and so conveying an impression of the distribution of objects in physical space. But seen objects tend to take their *time* relatively uniformly: they endure. On the other hand, auditory data take up space quite evenly by suffusing the local atmosphere; they yield most of their information through the temporal irregularities of onset and termination, of pitch and timbre and loudness. But these two senses don't simply split up space and time symmetrically between them: there is a better account of time in vision—as when we judge a runner's speed by contrasting the figure's progress with its fixed ground—than there is of space in hearing.

Like darkness and like death, silence is an absence that is charged with fear and need. An absence is no void, it is a quite particular negative presence. So important to us is sound in all its variety that its absence comprises a whole richly textured anti-world. Philosophical writers on silence have concentrated on that particular range of this antiworld that is the absence of the word, but primary silence underlies more than speech, more than all of speech and music put together. There is a deep though rarely acknowledged need for a sonic background in everyone's life, a background whose content remains unanalysed, below the threshold of awareness, but that stretches virtually without interruption from birth to death.

Donald A. Ramsdell has written: "[Awareness of background noise maintains] our feeling of being part of a living world and contribute[s] to our own sense of being alive. . . . We are not conscious of the important role which these backgrounds play in our comfortable merging of ourselves with the life around us, because we are not aware that we hear them. Nor is the deaf man aware he has lost these sounds; he only knows that *he feels as if the world were dead.*"

We speak of "dead silence" and of "deathly stillness." Silence is a death, because sound is movement and movement is an inalienable aspect of life. Background sound, the sound that is the unconsidered by-product of everyday comings and goings in the world around us, gives the world a texture of microactivity. It constitutes a kind of protodiscourse whose message is that we are not alone, that our flow of energy is answered, confirmed, sustained by other energies flowing around us, that the world is a place where a dialogue of vitality can be established. Music nowadays is used at least as much for background as for foreground, providing predictable continuity of animation to alleviate the anxiety of silence, an anxiety that has its roots in the fear of death. The occasional oases of silence golden and blessed that we all need from time to time are not respite from background sound but from noise, sound that is intrusive, untimely, or chaotic. Noisiest of all is perversely ordered sound, that of the neighbor's stereo for example, since order, whether relevant to our needs or not, always snaps awareness to attention.

Sound swells and recedes; it is intermittent and transient. This is because it is a consequence of the activity of things and not of all their activity at that: only of activity that is resisted in certain ways. Only when things bump into other things or rub against them do we hear sounds; or it may be that what we hear is the air itself pushing past a resistance, as when it whistles past a cornice or the mouthpiece of a flute. Thudding and smashing result from the uncompromising impact of mass on mass (a wine glass hits the floor and shatters: sounds will often bring news of abrupt endings). When two masses grudgingly negotiate a way past each other we may hear rasping, creaking, and squealing. Things are not always coming up against each other in these ways. We can see them whether they move or not, but we can hear them only when they move, and some of the things we most need to know about never break a total silence.

The command "be still" links images of silence and immobility. To be motionless is to be soundless. Our surroundings are as decisively differentiated by differing rates of motion as by different shapes and sizes, and sound has a necessary connection with the world's unquiet, with its looseness and free play—its process and vitality—and with our looseness in it.

Something thuds into a listener's awareness on hearing a mattock bite into a root. Other sounds slide over awareness or rub along it, or scratch or saw into it. A sound can soothe, or it can grate or seem to strike a blow; some sounds are deliberate acts of violence. Each sound has a life history which listeners follow by focusing a range of themselves into an adaptively variable stream. Even when it is reluctant, hearing is a fine-grained, evolving participation in what the source of the sound is going through. We are to a degree continuous across the intervening air with what moves with us in one commonality of vibration, because the sounding air has been galvanized by the source of the sound into acting as a vibrant connective tissue. One range of the listener is the struck and vibrating brass of the bell, while another stands aside to consider and pass judgment. The directness of the connection gives sound its intimate, unignorable quality. Crooning mother and listening infant re-create the recent union of their bodies.

Noise is a concept rooted in the domain of sound rather than sight, because the promiscuity with which sound addresses itself to appropriate and inappropriate receptors alike means that we must so often hear things we do not want to hear, whereas we can look the other way, or close our eyes, when we see something unpleasant or superfluous. (And since listening doesn't necessarily give itself away by the orientation and attitude of the listener's body, as looking does, we may know things we have heard, or

24

overheard, without it being known that we know.) Our auditory defenselessness casts us often in the role of victim, our privacy invaded by someone else's stereo or car horn.

And to hear a sound is to be involved: detachment comes more easily to seeing than to hearing. The difference between signaling an intention to pass on the highway by flashing headlights from high beam to low or by blowing the horn is the difference between a request and a demand. To hear is to be touched, moved perhaps, or even driven, often by what we cannot immediately locate and label: the ear, according to Nietzsche, is the "organ of fear." "What was that?" is more often the alarmed response to a hissing, or to a thud or a snapping and snuffling than it is to the glimpse of a shape, for most of the time to see something is to know where and what it is.

We associate the natural world primarily with the visible world; the world of sound is the great alternative. The link between sound and the supernatural is profound and widespread: ethnographer Anthony Jackson reports that "a deaf ritual specialist is an anomaly whereas a blind one is common enough." Possibly sound—like the gods a powerful unseen presence—is an unacknowledged model for our concept of the otherworldly. Feelings at once of oneness and of mystery can accompany the sensations of hearing: oneness because sound subordinates issues of distance and direction to those of energy—it surrounds the hearers and synchronizes them with one range of its source's activity; mystery because this range of activity is rarely tied in any inherent and necessary way to what matters about the size and shape of its source.

With sound it is not appearance that surrounds and invades us; it is that other principle, which believers call spirit, that is concerned with the animation of things. If we are believers, then we can believe that the spirit is moving us in our ritual music. Ritual sound makes the transcendent immanent. It is at the same time ours, our own sounds pressing in around us and running through us like a vital current of belief, molding us into a living interior that is proof against the unbelieving emptiness that lies around.

All human sounds are potentially communicative, even the unintended ones. The next few paragraphs go through a number of such sounds arranged in an order that runs from the fortuitous to the purposeful: from sounds that are the unintended consequences of actions that originated in other purposes, to those that are the would-be causes of actions. There are the scuffling and scraping sounds that are the inadvertent and incidental by-product of the body's passing encounters with its surroundings. Doorknobs turning, branches snapping under foot advertise our presence not only to others but to ourselves as well, for we keep ourselves company with these small reminders that we are present and going through the motions. This is the major range of sounds that must be suppressed when we operate by stealth. Both hunter and hunted work at gliding over surfaces rather than meeting them sharply and directly.

Other inadvertently generated sounds, such as wheezing and snoring, come from within the body and involve interference of one kind or another with breathing. Ordinary speaking and singing occupy only a small segment of the full range of possibilities for exploiting this source of expressive energy. Such explicitly expressive performances as laughing, crying, and groaning occupy a territory that falls between and overlaps with both the spontaneous and the calculated.

Signals intended to achieve an effect may either come from within the body, as does a street vendor's cry, or involve attacking some outside object, such as a bell. (Electric sirens show this signaling function fulfilled by a mechanism in which both effective force and resistance are external to the body.) The primates stay with man this far with their branch-shaking and their cries of warning or conviviality, but they don't make the quantum leap to speech, except, apparently, under duress. As a special class of signal, speech consists of suggestions and directions for action, but action in a restricted sense, for words exhort listeners (and readers) to engage initially in the special class of inner activity called thinking—whatever outward action may succeed the thought. By way of establishing a basis for discussing the most characteristically human elaborations of sound—speech and music—the next chapter proposes a model of the expressive function of the voice.

Chapter Two

VOICE

THE VOICE is one of the two major ways people are present to each other, complementing the look of the body's surface. Mostly we project ourselves, and compose each other, as syntheses of the two. But we believe, perhaps on the principle that seeing is believing, that its visible form of presence, its Field 1 phase, is what the self should ultimately be referred to. Substantial and abiding, it even survives the self for a time, in the form of an unsatisfactorily soundless corpse.

Yet many people are exclusively voices to us, on the radio or on the telephone, for example, our dealings with them centered in what they say and how they say it, and we know these people far better than we know those we know by sight alone. Of the two presences, the voice is the more intimately social one. Some reasons for this were urged in Chapter 1: the vagueness about distance characteristic of sound in effect draws the listener closer to its source; and listening is necessarily participation, stressing commonality with the source rather than difference from it.

The two forms of presence can project contradictory identities. An urge to fill in the picture may cause us to imagine faces and bodies to go with those disembodied radio and telephone voices, and any eventual confrontation of such a construct with reality is likely to be a shock, as when, for example, a piping voice is found to issue from a hulking body. Piping, avoluminous voices provide the same sort of hurdle to the ambitions of their owners that a spindly body might; and dim spirits may feel rebuked and upstaged by their own organ tones.

A number of different human sounds, the voice among them, result from the stratagem of tapping into the primary activity of breathing, and so, like a mill wheel in a stream, feeding off energy that is already available and in place. Among the other analogously produced sounds, some, like those of coughing and throat clearing, are side effects of actions whose purpose is not to produce sound, but the acoustic spin-off may have communicatory consequences anyway, at the very least in attracting attention. Throat clearing can be displaced from its original purpose and transformed into an admonitory statement. Sneezing, snoring, snorting interrupt the flow of air at the nose instead of the larynx; wheezing and gasping are protovocalizations, gasping exceptionally taking place on the intake, and this is a reminder of what is at once a deflating irony and a lesson in efficiency, that all our spoken eloquence, all our arias, and all our prayers are qualifications of the waste-removal phase of breathing.

Among all these sounds the voice is first in importance, presumably because of the wide range of precisely controllable variability it puts at its owner's disposal.

VOCALIZATION MAY be thought of as a freely manipulable representation and advertisement of the life that underlies it.

Any organism's survival is a matter of acting judiciously on the distinction between what is of the body and what lies outside it, and one of the basic ways this distinction is experienced, though not the only way, is as a dialogue between its two terms, between the body's force and the world's resistance; between the body's expansive activities of foraging, hunting, eating and drinking, and interacting with others and the variety of partially yielding resistance the world offers to them. Or force and resistance may be assigned the other way around, the body put in the position of defending itself against invasion from the outside.

Just as life emerges, in the model sketched above, from a primordial dialogue between force and resistance, so does the voice issue from the fluttering resistance of the larynx to the force exerted by the diaphragm on the spent air in the lungs. In the most blandly literal sense, the voice is expression, a pressing outward past the partially yielding obstacle of the vocal folds.

The dialogue between diaphragm and larynx can be thought of as a symbolic displacement to the body's interior of the interface between self and world, a displacement that has a strategic advantage over its original because, in this wholly embodied form, outside and inside are both inside where the self gets to play both sides of the game. (Musical instruments can be thought of as a re-displacement outward beyond the body's surface of this symbolic self/other interface; see Chapter 7).

The resulting signal, the sound of the voice, can be read as the self's sonic miming of its situation in the world. Thus the voice executes a power play. It enacts a symbolic takeover in which the confrontation between self and other is transformed from its real-life status of fatality, an irreducible given, to that of a ludic performance that can be entered into—or dropped out of—and shaped at will.

We cannot choose to have no visual appearance. No sooner do we make ourselves scarce in one place than we abound in another. But we can choose to have no auditory appearance at all simply by remaining silent, and this imparts a special quality to the moment we do commit ourselves to speech, or song, or any other sound. The voice strikes out beyond the way things are; it is always a performance reaching beyond the self-evident, a manifestation of will and intention. Even indifference becomes a performance when it is voiced.

Anything at all—a stab wound, news from the east, catching sight of a rainbow—that has bearing on the relationship between self and other can be reflected in the vocal representation of the threshold between them. It can be an anticipated situation or a remembered one. The occasion need not be external to the body: the other may manifest itself in the form of a visceral sensation. The perspective might be panoramic, taking in the vocalizer's life situation as a whole; more typically it is sharply focused on the immediate, transient situation, as in the case of a cry of pain. Here the resistance offered by the tightened vocal folds stands proxy for the pain itself, and the drive to be free of it assumes the form of air pressure built up against the blockage, as though to expel it. The pain may be relieved; what is actually expelled is a cry that is a portrait of agony.

We may moan over burnt toast or the world's folly, or pass over both in silence, but there is always this primitive music available when we choose to use it for representing the encounter between anything that seems to bear on our well-being and our resources of vital resiliency for dealing with it. Our sighs and bellows translate the flow and balance of energy at the threshold of the self into a new form, that of variations in volume, resonance, pitch, rhythm, and tempo projected out of an inner dialogue between physical force and resistance.

This inarticulate, preverbal music of mood and intent is a constant undercurrent in speech and can be understood even by those who have not completely mastered the language being spoken, like these small children in a novel by Toni Morrison: "Sometimes [grownups'] words move in lofty spirals; other times they take strident leaps, and all of it is punctuated with warm-pulsed laughter. . . . The edge, the curl, the thrust of their emotions is always clear. . . . We do not, cannot, know the meanings of all their words. . . . So we watch their faces, their hands, their feet, and listen for the truth in timbre." In literary studies "voice" may be used to refer to just this kind of truth as it is soundlessly implied by a written text.

Automatically and instinctively we all submit the melody of speech to a kind of instantaneous musical analysis. Affect is deduced by assessing the balance of force and resistance expressed in timbre, on a scale from breathiness to strangulation. A weak flow of air is the analogue of a low level of confidence in the vocalizer, whereas urgency and aggressiveness are conveyed by forceful and ample exhalation. In the 1850s Herbert Spencer wrote about the voice as an index of attitude and said of this same correlation: "The force with which [certain muscles of the chest and abdomen] contract is proportionate to the intensity of the feeling experienced. Hence, a priori, loud sounds will be the result of strong feelings." Of course, strong pressure from the diaphragm can only be converted to persuasive levels of volume by firm resistance.

The degree of open resonance of the tone in chest and head also correlates with the vocalizer's degree of self-assurance.

The breathiness produced by weak laryngeal occlusion suggests a lack of strong engagement with the outside world, while clamping down on the breath, with the resulting choked sound, conveys repression. Alan Lomax has compiled some evidence to show that "the relative severity of a culture's sexual code determine[s] the degree of tension to be heard in the voices of its favored singers."

The analysis opens out beyond timbre to encompass the wider "musical" ranges of tempo, rhythm, and melody as well. A varied melodic contour in the speaking voice goes with alertness and flexibility; steadiness of rhythmic flow suggests steadiness of purpose. Rapid tempo conveys urgency.

Clearly any inflexibly schematic application of these correspondences is bound to be misleading because there is too much play/"play" in the whole arrangement. Any of these "musical" dimensions can be consciously manipulated in order to persuade others, or ourselves to start off with, that we are stronger or weaker than we really are, or more or less beset. The audible range of appearance is yet more malleable than the visible.

The deepest layer of satisfaction in vocal expressivity may be the illusory sense of control it gives us over what it stands proxy for, our situation in life, a control far greater than that we exercise over the real thing (and this is probably the motivation underlying all such displacements, such as symbolizing). The vocal threshold is right there at our disposal; the vicissitudes of life are not.

A baby's first cry can be thought of as a move to control what must feel to it like a dangerous situation. The baby is itself at this point the entire universe as far as it can tell, and its first cry animates the territory around it without acknowledging anything or anyone in it, for its voice is available to it before it has any idea there is a separate world out there. But this solipsistic universe appears to be fragmenting into rebellious elements as it becomes aware of hunger, cold, glare—this is not the way things were where it came from—all the aspects of an incipient otherness. The baby first discovers alterity within itself, and the sound of its voice blooming stridently around it is evidence of its power to take command, if only by proxy, of the entire self/other complex.

Solitary vocalizing will continue, in the form of talking and humming, long after the baby has acquired a dualistic adult sense of itself as an animate particle suspended in a circumambient world. People are their own most loyal listeners, for the sound of their own voices is a message to themselves as well as to others, a message of self-confirmation and self-sufficiency. And vocalizers sound so much better to themselves, on the whole, than other people do, so much more resonant and immediate (though hearing ourselves as others hear us, in the form of a recording of our voices played back to us, can produce a shriveling of the sense of self-esteem).

Hearing the sound of their own voices returns vocalizers to themselves in a new form, with benefit to their sense of consequentiality, for the sound, while completely unlike their physical selves in its radical immateriality, still is uniquely their own and is heard only as and when they cause it to be heard. They set up a loop, a closed circuit in which kinesthetic and auditory sensations confirm each other.

When we hum to ourselves, we divide ourselves in two, into sound producers and listeners, and two is company. The greater part by far of the world's music is produced by solitary hummers and whistlers for no one's consumption but their own. As will be detailed in Chapter 7, musical instruments enlarge the loop, bringing outside matter and new manipulative skills into it and in so doing enlarge still further the performer's sense of practical competence and consequence in the larger world.

People often turn to musical courage in vaguely threatening situations, alone at night, for instance, on a street with no working street lights. The expression "whistling in the dark" makes of this sort of thing the classic instance of objectively futile braggadocio. Worse than futile perhaps, if the sound betrays one's presence and position to a would-be assailant. But the sonic loop does generate a sustaining sense of inviolable self-sufficiency. And the associations of the particular melody whistlers choose may take them further still, lighting up the street and peopling it with imaginary friends and performers.

Pendant to whistling in the dark is singing in the shower: in situations that are secure to begin with, self-generated sound may function as self-celebration. The shower stall is a warm moist womb where it is safe to be naked and open and its inhabitants may regress to the infantile stage when they were everything. But this new womb has better resonating characteristics than the original one, better than almost any other readily accessible space in fact, and with enhancement of the voice goes enhancement of self-esteem. Especially since no potential critics are visible.

People who sing to themselves, in or out of the shower, are self-enfolded in resonance that leaves appearance and location behind. They sense themselves as a diffused happening that does not depend for its validation on this or that outside event or object or consideration, a flow with no pronounced sense of before and after, of first this and then that. In Hinduism, intoning the mantra *Om* is a means of achieving union with the universe; but people who hum or whistle to themselves can achieve a temporary omniscience, since they are provisionally both self and other; or, what perhaps amounts to the same thing, they achieve a temporary return to that stage of infantile consciousness in which no division is made between within and without and the world is the resonance of self. They enter Field 3.

A B A B Y ' S cry of demand is the sound of a point aspiring to extension.

Vocalizing is a bid for control that can have two ranges. Above I have claimed that control over the larynx represents symbolic control over the threshold between self and other: that is the first range. In a shift in direction, the sound itself—shriek or sigh or level tone—disembodies that threshold, diffusing what began as a charged point outward through a physical space that may contain hearers. If it does, then the solipsistic sound loop is broken to include them, and vocalizing becomes a move to cause them to resonate with the vocalizer's situation, to become in a diluted sense one with it. This is the second range. It is a move by the self to occupy the awareness of others with the self's local act of taking possession of its otherness. About as soon as a baby discovers the existence of other people it learns that it can manipulate them with its voice. Hearing generally is entering into an ambient process and perceptually moving along with it, and the social use of the voice invites others to this kind of sympathetic involvement in our lives.

Sound spaces are short-lived inflated containers like soap bubbles, defined by the common resonance of what they contain. Any interesting sound draws listeners into a circle around its source; perhaps the throw of the voice set elastic physical limits to the space occupied by the first human polity. In any case the voice does stake out a kind of territorial claim for its owners to this space vibrating when and as they choose. In chaffinch, wren, reed warbler, and many other species of songbird this, along with attracting a mate, is its primary function. A portable stereo carried down a city street aims at something similar. Squalling babies or yapping puppies can seem to take up more room than large but silent people because of the urgency with which they diffuse their presences through their surroundings.

Linguistic convention has us speaking *to* each other, and so misleads us. Instead we speak each other, sing each other, are sung and spoken *by* each other; we are continuous with what moves as we do: we are one with it, in however attenuated a sense. Heard cries and utterances are surges of shared living. Submitting to a voice is never a neutral experience and brings with it a wide range of sensations from that of serenity to sharp irritation.

Certain rare voices have the power to invade, fill, and overmaster a listener, crowding out his independence of judgment. Elias Canetti describes the effect of a lecture by Karl Kraus:

> When he sat down and began to read, I was overwhelmed by his voice, which had something unnaturally vibrating about it, like a decelerated crowing. But this impression quickly vanished, for his voice instantly changed and kept changing incessantly, and one was very soon amazed at the variety that he was capable of. . . . The auditorium was enormous, yet a quivering in his voice was imparted to the entire space. Chairs and people seemed to yield under this quivering; I wouldn't have been surprised if the chairs had bent. The dynamics of such a mobbed auditorium under

the impact of that voice—an impact persisting even when the voice grew silent—can no more be depicted than the Wild Hunt. But I believe that the impact was closest to this legendary event. Imagine the army of the Wild Hunt in a concert hall, trapped, locked up, and forced to sit still, and repeatedly summoned to its true nature.

We can be ruled, nations sometimes have been ruled, by a voice rather than by the words it spoke.

At the point that purely expressive cries become cries of greeting or warning, the threshold where individual selfhood meets the outside is transformed into a new front of shared concerns. The resulting new unit, We, reconciles the physical separation of the individuals making it up with whatever they share in the way of needs and interests. Partners in conversation are at once apart—physically and perceptually quite distinct from each other, each with access to only a limited sector of his or her surroundings and with a distinct history and program of needs—and together in a new synthetic place, the location of their sympathetic resonance in common.

Chapter Three

―――――

WORDS

―――――
――――
―――

THE HUMAN domestication of sound in the form of speech has taken us farther than our mastery of fire or tools or any of our other conquests. It permeates them all.

In other species vocal sound is a sparsely settled territory, populated by no more than a few squatters here and there in the form of instinctively programmed signaling cries. Our most distinctive initiative as a species has been the massive colonization of this territory with significances of our own making, references to an open-ended array of relevant but not self-evident possibilities, such as: things as it is opportune to see them as having been; things as they may be but elsewhere; and things as we would like them to turn out; or as they may turn out whatever we do; or as they will not turn out if we can help it.

With this potential, it is a clear waste of resources to talk about the way things are right before our eyes and we spend little time doing so, though conversation must be referable, however indirectly, to the identity of the speakers involved and what their situation is, if it is to make sense. Speech articulates the social synchrony achieved through vocalizing and listening with an indirect claim on a realm beyond the reach of the senses, and it does so in ways that are directly furthered by the nature of sound and our control over it.

Moreover, the absent is present, as it is represented in speech, with a kind of forcefulness alien to visual representation—despite the lack of any resemblance between the sounds of speech and what they are about—because of the peremptory immediacy of sound.

Since the archaeology of sound has no hard subject matter earlier than the late nineteenth century (phonetic alphabets are not that much older than acoustical recordings relative to the antiquity of speech, and they are a lot softer as evidence), we are left free to speculate that the first step in the campaign to dilate the present that led eventually to speech may have been some remote ancestral urge to develop more situationally specific, situationally adaptive cries to attract attention, signal mood, and issue commands or warnings ("interjectional" theories of the origin of speech are as old as Democritus).

All primates have a repertory of such cries. A cry of warning, for example, could have been modified by lips and tongue, once they had evolved the flexibility to do the job, into phonological variants associated specifically with, for example, "leopard" or "fire." The larynx is a relatively old idea in evolutionary terms, being common to many orders, but one reason chimpanzees cannot speak is that they lack the physical capacity for phonation that first appeared in humans.

This development can be accounted for by extending the model for vocalizing developed in the last chapter. There it was suggested that the relationship between force and resistance at the sounding larynx mimes the corresponding relationship between self and other, that vocalizing thus enacts a taking charge by proxy on the part of the self of its situation, and that addressing the resulting sound to listeners is a bid to resonate them with a token for that situation and so a bid for a measure of control over them.

Speech further extends the territory brought under the vocalizer's control. The components of the force/resistance: self/ other model that undergo centrifugal expansion with the development of speech are "other" and its parallel, "resistance." In the case of the utterance "fire" or "leopard" mentioned above, the underlying cry of warning remains what it is for an inarticulate primate: it mimes danger to the self from something "other" in a sharp confrontation of forced air and laryngeal resistance. Just as leopards and fires are particular articulations of the broad real-life category of dangerous situations, so some aboriginal equivalent of the sounds "leopard" and "fire" would have articulated the general-purpose warning cry with patterns of subtle additional resistance, interrupting and releasing the stream of vocal sound at the surface of the body just before it escaped control. An analogy would be that other transformative interruption that takes place when the variable resistances of film to a beam of light directed at it result in the flow of images projected onto a screen beyond. The undifferentiated image of menacing otherness conveyed by the inarticulate cry takes on the specificity of fangs and claws or smoke and flame through the addition of a new layer of resistance at the vocalizer's mouth to the stream of air rising from the lungs, at this point already broken up into sound waves by the vocal folds. Speakers and listeners are now aligned with each other in confrontation with an other whose precise nature is known to all present, even though it may remain invisible to as many as all but one of them.

What emerged from the fleeting stoppage and shaping of the flow of vocal sound that produced the proto-"leopard" phonation was a sticking point in the stream of thought, an image for the screen of the mind. Robert Frost wrote of the sentence that it is "a sound in itself on which other sounds called words may be strung": the message is still rooted in its prearticulate layer, the "sound in itself." And still at the center of it all is the primitive self-confirmation of the sound of the speaker's own voice.

This is one way to reconstruct the breakthrough to representations that do not have the look of what they stand for; however this breakthrough came about, it was crucial to the emergence of speech. A logical next step would have been using these new sounds in the absence of actual fires and leopards, at first perhaps in the shared recollection of terrors experienced before and then in anticipating possible terrors to come, in order to prepare for them. The new oral, phonemic resistance became the resistance of a new range of the other, of what speakers and listeners could not see or touch or hear. If the shaping of phonemes did not actually bring the past, the future, and the elsewhere into being it is the origin of their vast expansion in Field 2.

In one way this would have been a trivially easy step to take: compared to what it takes to represent something in a drawing, for example, the outlay of time and energy that it takes to produce an utterance is slight. But psychologically the shift is enormous, entailing as it does a radical realignment in imagination of speaker and listener. Even the most primitive snort of alarm alerts the members of the pack to a presence that cannot yet be seen by all of them; but now they are asked to orient themselves in relation to what none of them could see if they tried.

Probably we will never know how it took place, but in one way or another speech detached itself from the immediate reference of the primate signaling cry; for in even the most ordinary conversation speaker and listener locate themselves in a manifold whose dimensions extend vastly beyond those of the physical present in which the conversation is taking place, taking in states of affairs, whether wished for, or feared, or simply attested to, in a meta-sensory range including past, future, and elsewhere. In Charles Hockett's scheme of design features found in communications systems, this is called "displacement." This is Field 2, the "other" vastly expanded over the version of it that the senses report in Field 1. Its contents are defined with a degree of specificity that rivals that available in Field 1, but the constraints governing action here are far looser. The greatest ancestral migration, the most heroic of ancient journeys, was the one that led our early ancestors out from the here and now and into the dangerous freedom of Field 2.

The mechanism for the additional level of resistance at the top of the breathing tube that made the expanded "other" possible is borrowed from the top of the food tube where it continues to supervise a flow that is moving in the opposite direction, preferably not at the same time. As Christopher Collins has observed, teeth, tongue, jaw, and lips, all of which evolved for the essentially aggressive acts of sucking and biting and chewing are here put to work on spent air instead of food and drink. This is preadaption, in the language of Darwinism. The result is vocal tone nibbled into phonemic morsels meant to be expelled rather than swallowed. There is plenty of air to go around, so breathing is normally a placid, cyclic affair, but as it moves into the new hunting grounds of Field

2, shaped into speech by the weaponry of the more competitive and destructive activity of eating, it takes on an aggressive, expansionist character.

The new layer of sound shaping gives rise to a complex and difficult internal dialogue, unique to humans, between depth and surface, throat and mouth, and this corresponds to a problematic doubleness in human nature—crudely, the duality of feeling and thought, or of heart and head, oppositions that are closely related to those of body and mind, Fields 1 and 2. More will be said about this in the next chapter, which will attempt a contrastive ordering of the traits associated with speech and song.

WHEN I say to someone, "Let's stop off for coffee and maybe a roll," I give my present flesh and blood situation a tentative and shadowy extension. Like the pseudopod of an amoeba, this extension could take hold and establish a new situation toward which the present one would then flow. By my act of addressing him, I will my listener to extend his situation in the same direction, working out of our covibrancy in the sound of my speaking voice; something similar would happen if I were to take him by the elbow in order to turn him toward some sight of interest. In fact, my proposal may be accompanied by some spillover of energy into gestures that mime the urgency and some of the content (such as the direction we will need to walk to get to the coffee shop) of what I say; in any case, the way I say it—the timbre, rhythm, and pitch contour of my voice—convey whatever hope and intensity I have invested in my suggestion.

The sidewalk where we stand, the angle at which the light strikes the buildings around us, my partner pausing and looking my way, the pattern of tension in my body turned toward him and the sensations of contracting and pushing in diaphragm, throat, and mouth that go with saying these words: all these sensations and many more are aspects of my grip on the moment. The words themselves point to a possible future in which all this would have dissolved.

But at the time I make my proposal, having coffee is at some level still a part of present reality. It has somewhat the status of the traffic light that is a number of yards away but still visible from where we stand, with the crucial difference that it is not present to our senses, or even imagined in a vivid way. Things like the smell of the coffee and the roll, or the feeling of sitting back at ease, and the rest of what belongs to a coffee break are present in this extension of where we stand in the most shadowy way, if at all. Rather than being the evocation of a scene—and it takes hold almost the instant it is spoken, certainly before such a scene could be imagined in any detail—my invitation is a tropism, a direction of flow for the present moment's tension.

The process of maintaining the best possible picture of what there is, over many focal lengths and degrees of stability, creates something like an atmosphere opening out around the moment and around the space occupied by the body, only a small part of it conscious at any one time. It goes where we go, changing with circumstances. At its center is the process of integration we call the self.

Fields 1 and 2 interpenetrate. This atmosphere is maintained by sightings over two intercommunicating ranges: the dense and immediate range of the senses (this traffic light, this sidewalk), and a rarefied metasensory one whose primary sensory occasion is the sound of the voice (let's stop off for coffee). Though each gesture in this second range begins as a private thought, the range itself interpenetrates to varying degrees those of other individuals, because it is rooted in the interindividual coordination of mood and action won by the voice.

In Field 1, the other, older range of awareness, we touch, smell, taste, and see things all in a vital solitude. But speech acts like a new, communitywide sense modality whose true territory begins where that of the senses that orient us as individuals stops, extending the awareness of participants beyond the immediately verifiable. The great novelty of this new faculty, considered as a sense, is that it synthesizes its own stimuli, though the basic ingredients of these stimuli are all known in advance in the form of a shared vocabulary: literally speaking there *is* no coffee, no roll; yet my conversational partner and I are both earnestly directing our attention toward an object identifiable with nothing else.

The validity of a human community is the willingness of its individual members to leap where they cannot look, to act on the basis of the memories and perceptions and syntheses of others as these are reported in speech. In this way they can act as though they have seen what they have not in fact seen, been where they have never been, and they can form themselves into novel dynamic configurations (walking, for example, toward the coffee shop instead of standing here talking about it), so they can remain fundamentally one in their dispersion across the terrain.

Going along with all this emphasis on the extrinsic and centrifugal is a dimming and thinning of the sense of here and now. Field 2 is a great leveler: here the perceptible present is no more real than the absent past, future, and elsewhere, and very likely it is accorded lower status than they are. A conversation may be thought of as a small conspiracy to escape being stuck fast in the midst of what there merely is. The conversation's center is a version of the physical present that is never robustly asserted but is a silent inference from the evolving web of circumstance woven by the conversation, a nexus of potential movements of approach and evasion. Reality can come to seem like a spike driven into the middle of this extended consciousness, nailing it to the moment.

The occasion for seeing or tasting anything or for saying something like "How about coffee?" is always a unique and unrepeatable point along the perceiver's or speaker's trajectory. Each remark, whether it deals with coffee or the intricacies of semiotic theory or what fine weather we're having, is pulled out of us as speaker by our sense of a surrounding vacuum, of the uneasy indeterminacy of our situation. Speech, even monologue, is a dialogue with emptiness, an optimistic effort to fill in the blanks of possibility in the metasensory range of the speaker's awareness, the great human project to control what cannot be sensed or handled.

Field 2 is no passive container for thought. It has the character of a chronically unanswerable metaquestion drawing out of us remarks, conjectures, questions proper (at moments when the metaquestion comes into sharp local focus), exclamations, the unspoken versions of all these in a compulsive, unceasing stream that is still there, flowing underground, when we dream. The existence of Field 2 encourages a pervasive background conviction that there has got to be more to it all than the This the senses report—because each time we speak or simply imagine there *is* more, a reality beyond appearance. And the possibility of achieving a mathematical purity of form in Field 2, unresisted by the obduracies of Field 1, encourages giving that ultrareality a Utopian cast.

The original predicate is the other, and the self is the subject of subjects. Self and other, pressed into each other in an unbroken flow of mutual negotiation and definition, is syntax before speech, the syntax of organic existence. Speech extends duality to the problem of making public percepts that, for any of a variety of reasons, are accessible to the senses of the original perceiver only: "This coffee is cold." In an instantaneous take, a sentence, most distinctively human of actions, locates the original subject, the speaker, relative to a subsidiary subject, "coffee," the subject of the sentence. This is fitted out with directions for how it is to be taken in the form of a predicate, a provisional defining other—in an extended sense a location: a quality of temperature, or perhaps of difference or sameness, or motion, or bulk.

Remarks and questions follow one another in the course of a conversation in a kind of metavisual scanning, each remark dissolving into the next by association ("Have them get you another one") or jump cut under pressure ("You're about to knock the saucer off with your elbow"). From a physical vantage point, each remark is perfectly insubstantial, an ephemeral flow of energy states; each consumes itself in the saying to make room for the next. The resulting movement from topic to topic is more free even than the scanning movements of the eyes as they slide from the elbow to the saucer to the floor, because it is not limited, as the gaze is, to what there is out there but synthesizes its own landscape.

It is as easy to refer in conversation to the planet Jupiter as it is to Brooklyn: nothing prevents them from being set side by side in the same sentence, as they are here. Two thousand years ago or next week are as accessible to sentence making as is yesterday. Unlike the situation in the outside world, to approach some things in this space is not at all to move away from others: in the words of a Chinese proverb, "How is it far if you think it?" Word work is a kind of pragmatic surrealism that permits us to project in a hypothetical way linkages and sequences among tokens that are far different from those that actually obtain—and then, if it seems worthwhile, to work toward replacing the actual by the hypothetical in the real world. If/then is a more powerful tool than the wheel. Often remarks are testing and exploratory, but often they simply confirm what is known to everybody as part of the effort to establish a locus for the conversation common to all its participants. After all, to see the same things in the same way is to be in the same place. And so we navigate our lives by triangulating a flow of sightings with those of our conversational partners.

T H E R E   A R E   reasons for thinking that the characteristics of sound, and of vocal sound in particular, played an essential facilitating and shaping role in the evolution of speech, considered (as I have been considering it here) as a technique for achieving a flow of hypothetical alignments and realignments in the metasensory range of awareness I call Field 2. In what follows I will relate the nature of speech to the following attributes of sound: its perceptibility to a degree independent of the hearer's orientation; its independence of outside sources of energy; most important, its relative independence of the world in its aspect of spatial displacement and location; and, finally, its easy manipulability.

One advantage the voice has over gesturing, its strongest rival as a means for coordinating our dispersion, is that it does not use equipment needed for anything else. Vocalizing does not interfere with picking over things or clutching them, nor does it slow us down as we move about the landscape. In addition, vocal signals work as well at night as during the day, and they can be picked up by listeners however they are facing; they get around objects that would block visual signals.

49

These are compelling practical reasons for favoring the voice over the alternatives that address vision as a way of coordinating daily activities. If we imagine a primate that is committed to vocal signaling because of the special advantages just mentioned, and if we imagine this primate impelled by whatever combination of environmental stress and anatomical opportunity to expand its repertory from grunts of fear, bliss, and the like to more finely articulate evocations of leopards or figs or whatever occasions such feelings, then these new enriched signals will necessarily break with the original aspects of those occasions, leaving appearance behind.

This is because there is no way to make a sound resemble a leopard or a fig or any other physical entity. Whereas our innovative primate might allude to a leopard by imitating the leopard's roar, the fig resists this approach; and too much of the rest of what must figure in the primate's plans—from light to darkness, from the earth to the sky to growing things—is mute and still to make a rich inventory of it possible through the use of onomatopoeia. Perhaps our early ancestor was such a primate.

This primate might very well have been scratching pictures in the mud or on the walls of caves, and might very likely have made use of a variety of hand signals and other bodily gestures. But the primate is not likely to have started drawing pictures with no resemblance to their originals before speaking of those same things in syllables that had an only arbitrary connection with their references. The pictures and the utterances alike would have been concerned mainly, at the start, with the spatial aspect of the primate's surroundings, since that is the aspect with the most immediate bearing on well-being, and, with visual representations of such things, likeness, however schematic, is the path of least resistance.

It would require a special effort of the will to represent a person by drawing a horizontal line, or a leopard by a vertical one, and the result would annul the special feeling of power over the original that a likeness induces in both maker and viewer. With vocal representations, on the other hand, likeness is not a major option: it is largely ruled out by the crossover in modality from space to time. Representing a physical object by means of sound involves a move from stable configurations in space to variable rates of invisible oscillation.

The loss of one kind of power, the kind inherent in the resemblance of a token to its referent, is more than made up for by gains that are also attributable to detachment from appearances: nonlikenesses are both more generalizable and more freely combinable in novel configurations than are likenesses, and speech exploits both possibilities in reaching for a new kind of power. Precisely because the sounds produced by the voice have no spatial characteristics of their own, they can, if we choose, stand for anything in space, or for any place, or for everywhere or nowhere. In our general experience we hardly regard sounds as insignificant because they do not resemble physical things. We are conditioned to looking for the significance of sounds beyond the surface they themselves present, to, for example, the tree frog that experience tells us always makes that particular croak, a connection that only experience could make because the sound made by a tree frog and its appearance cannot be related in any other way.

It is no big step from this to relating sounds of our own invention and production to a new range of significances that we ourselves bring into being. Breaking with the look and the heft of things is a necessity in vocal communication, and on a massive scale we have made a virtue of it by capitalizing on a whole new range of manipulative possibilities that it opens up. Perhaps this was the punctuation of some hominid's equilibrium that produced human kind, consistent with the long-range trend in evolution toward greater and greater independence of particular niches in particular environments.

We evoke the unknown for each other as an extension of established categories: the vocabulary of speech is significant past experience with the juice of particularity squeezed out of it. To the extent any representation, visual or auditory or any other, resembles what it refers to it will resemble some particular instance, a cherry tree say, or, if the detail is finer still, the particular huge old cherry tree that grows in the backyard.

Conversely, to the extent it is independent of the details of the appearance of a particular instance it can refer to a family of them, including instances never experienced at firsthand, or to totally imaginary ones. The syllable "tree" could never resemble a plant of any description, let alone the cherry tree in the backyard, since its existence is in a different dimension from the one in which we apprehend plants, or, for that matter, physical objects generally, and so can evoke innumerable woody, branching entities dispersed through time and space. And the existence of symbols emancipated from appearance is an invitation to create further symbols for what could never have any appearance at all, such as the concept behind the word "appearance" itself.

Just about any representation of a tree can be moved around more freely than its original and set more freely in juxtaposition with other items. But the symbol that carries with it no reminders of what it refers to is marginally more manipulable than a likeness, because with it we feel no inhibitions about launching forth into transformations that would seem incongruous with either the original or something resembling it. The word "tree" is rootless, it casts no shadow and claims no place for itself in any actual landscape among rocks and hills and so can be brought into discussions of lumber and paper production with no wrenching sense of dislocation, or transfigured into the Tree of Life.

Arbitrary representations can be highly compressed in the interests of efficiency without the kind of loss that would affect a compressed likeness, and the compression of individual representations makes possible the compression of messages that compact several of them, with consequent savings on space or (and particularly in the case of voiced signals) time. Communication using such conventional signs can often move more swiftly than events and so move out in front of them.

Abstraction and generalization and compression can be characteristics of symbols addressed to any of the senses, but symbols shaped in sound can be manipulated with particular fluidity. No play could be freer than playing with air: the transition from the semisolid, close-textured body to insubstantial air is as abrupt as the one from the earth to the body. And vocal sound is flow detached from the world seen and touched. Sound is between things as air is, not of them; its invisible, weightless states are never in the way, they take up no room and leave no visible scars. In general we can articulate and perceive changes in these states more quickly than changes in patterns of light. Speech performs all the metamorphoses parodied in an illusionist's act—the materializations out of nowhere and the disappearances into thin air, the transformations of condition and number—at a fraction of the effort.

I N O N E perspective, speech appears as an expansion outward from the self lodged in its present; in another as an implosion into the amorphous inner life of thought. Speech may be preceded as well as sustained by this mode of displaced imaginary action that is still more free than speech, lacking its grammatical and other constraints and not limited to words but including visual and tactile and kinesthetic elements as well.

The experiences of thinking and hearing have more in common than do those of thinking and seeing. We do not, after all, say: "I can't see myself think," but we do say "I stopped to listen," just as we say "I stopped to think." Both thinking and listening are helped by suspending exploratory activity, whether physical or visual, directed toward our physical surroundings. Both are forms of engagement with a disembodied process: neither sounds nor thoughts are durable entities moving in relation to fixed spatial coordinates. Yet what we want our thoughts to give us is "the picture": thinking reaches for the quasi-visual fixity and certainty of understanding. If we do hear ourselves think it is a hearing that aspires to vision.

By means of the articulated sound of speech we can hear each other think. Since both sound and thought are disembodied processes, sound can shadow the moves of thought, even spur them on. It may be that there is as much thinking to be heard publicly as there is in part because we are physically able to articulate and hear so much: it may be that human thought moves as quickly and freely as it does because it is keeping pace with the lips and the tongue, which have evolved in ways that capitalize on the low inertia of air and of hearing.

Thought in its relatively elaborate human form was not preformed and waiting to be discovered before our species came along; its broad objectives, though, had been in existence since the formation of life: keeping watch over the relationship between organism and environment, preparing appropriate action, and, in social species, staying synchronized with the perceptions and intentions of others. Human thought is the pursuit of these age-old ends by new means, in a field vastly opened out by the emergence of a new means of communication. Articulated sound encouraged, besides swiftness, abstraction and free combinatoriality in the thinking that backed it up.

Sound does not itself range freely over past, future, and elsewhere, as thought does, but it is not tied to the visible present either, being itself invisible. In its detachment from Field 1, sound could sponsor an adaptively advantageous emancipation of thought from the state of affairs at any given moment, and the emancipation of its content from such constraints on physical movement as the one-way pull of gravity and the next-to, on-top-of, nearer-farther relationships of objects in space. Articulate sound did not invent abstract thought—there is evidence for such thinking in the behavior of speechless animals—but did encourage its vast expansion. Perhaps the Cartesian duality of mind and matter could be described as a duality of degrees of manipulability running from ideas to things, with the greater manipulability of ideas a function of the ease with which sound can be articulated.

Much thought is never communicated, and the thinkable is not restricted to the communicable. Much thought is the productive waste motion of trial and error; not all of it can be trimmed and fitted to the requirements of the available channels for communication. Some of it is kept deliberately secret.

But the communicable has greater survival value than the solipsistic in the long run, bearing as it does on collective action—past a certain point solipsistic thought would even have a loosening effect on the bonding of the community—and so we can suppose that the expansion of the human ability to think that distanced humans from the other primates followed from the increased possibilities for communicating thought that came with their more extensive and finer-textured exploitation of sound as a medium.

Giving upright posture, and the opposable thumb, and any other appropriate physical factors their due, and the synergy of their contributions to the result we call human, and the consequent difficulty of singling out any one of them for special comment, I would still urge a central role for sound in shaping human distinctiveness. For all the eloquence of gesture and receptiveness of clay, or blank walls, or sheets of paper, the sound of the human voice in its lability and linguability is the best patron thought has. On this view culture is to a very great extent a precipitate of vocal play. And the free play from which speech proceeds continues into the process of taking it in. Listeners are unlikely to give themselves completely to a conversation; rather they lend an ear and, like the readers of this book, hold the rest in actively skeptical reserve.

W H A T B E C O M E S of the force/resistance:self/other model of vocal communication when, in the case of writing, the word remains but the voice is still?

A movement away from the here and now is already evident in speech itself when it is compared to wordless cries, taking the form of expansion: the "other" dilates to become Field 2, taking in past, future, and elsewhere. This detachment is carried further in writing with the loss of the immediacy of a resonating voice. Here it is the share of the self and not the other that changes. But instead of expanding, as the other does in speech, the self in a written text shrinks back to become a silent record of its sonic embodiment in the speaking voice.

Once it had achieved its evolutionary conquest of thought, the voice (and so, incidentally, aspects of the self) could sometimes be in the way; in the way, in particular, of the impulse to preserve ideas for an indefinite time beyond the moment they are born— sound being evanescent—and to circulate them beyond the territory covered by the voice. Before electricity was introduced into domestic life, preservation mostly meant leaching all the juice and movement out of whatever was to be preserved. The sound of the voice, the essence of sound being movement, had to be sacrificed in the analogous project of preserving thought. So, by a process analogous to the one that makes prunes out of plums, writing leaches the voice out of articulated thought and converts what is left to a long, thin skeleton doubling back and back on itself along the page. This kind of toneless speech has the durability not only of skeletons but also of such utilitarian artifacts as cups and saucers. It keeps better than spoken utterances, travels better, and stores conveniently. It is the means of a very useful thing, an objective interindividual memory whose monuments are libraries and archives. This topic is touched on again in Chapter 6.

As valuable to us as the vital intimacy of the voice is, it can be in the way of enterprises besides those of preservation and dissemination. Some writing is in flight from the revealing sensuous immediacy of the voice before it is anything else, in its search for a more detached kind of control over its audience. "A Letter always feels to me like immortality because it is the mind alone without corporeal friend. Indebted in our talk to attitude and accent—there seems a spectral power in thought that walks alone"— this is something that Emily Dickinson wrote rather than said. Writing gets some of its authority from what it lacks, things like the scratchiness, the hesitancy, the lisp of particular speaking voices. Like the sound of a musical instrument considered as an alternative to the singing voice (on this point see Chapter 7), it lacks reminders of the fallible mortality, the life story, the sex of a particular speaker and so takes on a measure of oracular impersonality. Seeing, even seeing words, can be believing: people are in greater danger of believing everything they read than everything they pick up as hearsay. The written page is a neutral mask which in a crucial respect puts each writer on the same footing as any other. And the writer can indulge in the pleasures of holding forth from behind an impersonal persona without interruptions.

The concept in literary studies of "voice" was apparently created by the absence from written literature of the physical voice—it would have less play in studies of literature that is transmitted orally. "Voice" in this sense is not so much a presence as a quest for something to supplant an absence situated at the focus of vocabulary, phrasal rhythm, and the rest, like the resultant tone the ear sometimes extrapolates from two other tones sounded together.

In the matter of control, readers are at the balancing point with the writer: they have more control by far over the text's control over them than does any listener over a spoken message. They can pick the text up and put it down at their pleasure, and write whatever they choose in its margins. There is even something lightly illicit in readers' capacity to see unseen.

In particular, the whole question of the voice is up to them, and they can fill out the tracery on the page with resonance real or imaginary at their pleasure. In almost all cases, written texts have arrived at the page straight from the author's head, so that the texts' voices, in the sense of intonation and speed and so forth, are phantom voices. One result in particular cases is that readers could conceivably end up improving on anything an individual author could produce in a reading.

Chapter Four

WORDS AND MUSIC

H E N R Y P U R C E L L ' S song "Music for a while" begins with two self-exemplifying instantiations of the word "music":

Henry Purcell, "Music for a while" (Zimmerman 583/2), inserted in Oedipus *by John Dryden and Nathaniel Lee, act 3, scene 1. (Purcell's music was commissioned for a revival in 1692 and concerned only Dryden's share of the tragedy.) Reproduced here from the Gregg Press reprint (Ridgewood, N.J., 1965) of* Orpheus Britannicus, *3d ed. (London, 1721), vol. 2.*

A single pitch is maintained throughout both syllables. This would be unusual in any spoken version of the word, which would be likely to move through a continuously variable flow of pitch. This one pitch is given a surround of other stable pitches by the accompaniment, and as the song continues an experienced listener quickly hears the first of the two pitches as the center of a hierarchical system formed by them all, a closed and constantly recirculating set.

The word "music" ordinarily takes less than a second to say. Two seconds is a rough estimate for each of Purcell's settings of it here; if the word were spoken that slowly it would have a distinctly lugubrious effect. These two ranges overlap—the ranges for speed of declamation in speech and in song—but the range for song is much greater and it has a wide range of options at the "long" end of the spectrum all to itself.

This musical prolongation of a single word sung to one pitch has the effect of focusing attention on the sheer sonic quality of the voice, its timbre and resonance. The claims on attention of phonemes formed at the upper end of the tubular cavity from which speech issues, and along with them the claims of referential meaning, fade in relation to those of the physically more deeply centered resonances of the larynx, and this distribution of emphasis is reinforced by the share of attention a listener must give to the phoneme- and reference-free instrumental accompaniment.

SPEECH AND song are the two main ways people influence each other using internally impeded exhalation that issues in sound. Sorting out these two is no straightforward matter, because in practice their characteristics don't polarize cleanly: speech can't help involving the basic laryngeal mechanism; most songs use words. Yet even allowing for such in-between phenomena as Sprechgesang and rapping, most of the time most people familiar with the tradition will know which of the two they are dealing with (this book employs "speech" and "song" as they are commonly applied to European and European-derived musics and languages).

What are the signals that tell a Western listener that this is music, that speech? The situations in which we encounter the two tend to differ, and that is a help. The presence or absence of instruments is another indicator. But my premise here is that the distinction is rooted in two different ways we have of making and shaping vocal sounds. I propose a contrastive ordering of the auditory features that distinguish speech from song, and of the mechanisms producing them. I suggest further that the functions of song and speech form a loosely complementary pair corresponding to the pair formed by the physiological phenomena that generate their differing sensory surfaces.

It is important to acknowledge that this polarizing method imposes a false clarity on the subject. Singing and saying are in reality distributed along a continuum, and concentrating hard on contrastive features draws attention away from the rich, contradictory mix of these features typical of actual vocal performances. It slights, to take just one example, the role and the extent of redundancy in ordinary conversational speech. Incantatory speech (as found, for example, in southern African-American preaching) and expository song (as in recitative) wrongly take on the character of anomalies in this perspective.

But the distortion can serve purposes beyond those of reductive simplification. If the point of genres such as Sprechgesang and rapping—and their fascination for the analyst—lies precisely in their accommodation of contrasting tendencies, then an initial simple-minded binary clarity about those tendencies can perhaps yield a richer sort of clarity at a further stage of analysis, a more

exact and detailed picture than would otherwise be available of the
interplay of these tendencies over the full range of vocal practice.

Setting up this speech/song distinction entails identifying
those minimal features of each that cannot be varied without varying the essential nature of the entity, verbal or musical, of which
they form a part. It seems that notation might be a help here. As an
assumption, notation will concentrate on those features of the
entity it records that are indispensable to its reconstitution, and so
presumably fundamental to its nature.

Judging by Western musical notation, the specification of
pitch is essential to Western music (the fact that Hopi song, for
example, does not make use of discrete pitches can serve as a brake
on any tendency to universalize this point). Western scripts do not
allow the same conclusion to be drawn about the languages they
record. The written word "music," for example, simply leaves the
whole issue of pitch variability untouched. In actual practice the
word might be spoken to a virtually unlimited range of intonation
patterns without affecting its distinctively semantic (as opposed,
say, to its rhetorical) message. But these same intonation patterns
detached from the word "music" and vocalized by themselves are
an array of so many noninterchangeable "musical" entities. To vary
pitch is to vary the essential musical message but does not affect
the semantic core of a speech utterance (with the obligatory exception of tone languages), and this distribution of priorities is reflected in the notational systems of music and speech.

The crucial variables for speech are phonemes. Western alphabets are inventories of these minimal meaning-discriminating
ways of shaping sound, broken down roughly into vowels and consonants. Of the two, consonants have the greater power to convey
information (this is implied by the traditional etymology for the

62

Sanskrit word meaning consonant, "vyañjana," deriving it from a root meaning "revelative"). This is confirmed once again by notational practice: the alphabetical notation "msc," for instance, takes us closer to "music" than does "ui." Hebrew is an example of an alphabet restricted to signs for consonants.

Broadly speaking, vowels and consonants correspond, respectively, to the musician's timbre and attack characteristics. Music assigns important roles to these variables, but they are clearly secondary to pitch and rhythm, and musical notation pays no detailed attention to them. Despite "pizzicato," "marcato," and so forth, music has nothing in the area of attack characteristics to match the range and subtlety of such things as bilabial plosives and labiodental fricatives; in fact, one great service the words of songs provide their music is the variety of ways consonants afford of getting notes started.

Even so, song strongly tends to reverse linguistic priorities and favor vowels over consonants (the array of timbres produced by musical instruments might be seen as a lexicon of vowels belonging to a language that has shied away from any extensive commitment to consonants and, along with them, to referential meaning). Songs generally take longer to sing than their texts do to say, and the difference lies mainly in a musical inclination to linger over vowel sounds. Purcell's prolongation of the word "music," for example, focuses primarily on the "u" sound, secondarily on the "i," not at all on the rest, "msc." Recitative, most speechlike of the European genres of song, is to aria as consonant is to vowel. Speech regresses in song in the direction of the prearticulate—though far from subrational—cry, as its vowels expand in duration and volume and resonance. The rule of reason is maintained by the schematic handling of pitch, rhythm, and form.

Intonation (pitch variability) and phonetic articulation make up a contrastive pair of classes of minimal constituents central to, respectively, song and speech: substituting one phoneme for another alters the verbal meaning of a song without affecting its musical sense, the reverse holding for the alteration of pitch.

The anatomical sites for shaping these variables are different: singing elaborates the resonance of the body's center. Nobody lip-reads tunes: intonation, the music-intensive member of the pair, is generated deep in the mechanism for vocal sound production, in the larynx, while phonemes are formed at its upper end. (Philomel's musical eloquence issued from a mouth whose tongue had been torn out.) Among the two classes of phonemes, the vowels, the more "musical" of the pair, are resonated further back than the consonants, which are shaped by lips, teeth, tongue and palate. Both of these configurations can be interpreted as center/periphery oppositions.

In Chapter 2 a force/resistance:self/other model of the expressive working of the voice was proposed, according to which both self and other are represented in the encounter between exhalation and the tightened vocal folds and in this way brought symbolically under the vocalizer's control. Speech was presented in Chapter 3 as expanding the share of the other in this model through the mechanism of a new layer of resistance—lips, teeth, tongue—to exhalation. How does song fit into this scheme?

Speaking emphasizes articulation at the upper end of the vocal mechanism, where it is associated with a fine-textured manipulation of our picture of the other; in singing, the weight of emphasis shifts to the lower end. Adapted to the strengths and limitations of the larynx, this specifically musical articulation is a working of pitch, timbre, resonance, and amplitude that is, of course, far more detailed and far more schematic than anything found in the expressive cries that are the original product of this layer of vocalization, achieving an order of sonic complexity corresponding to that of verbal phonation. Yet it lacks any elaborate semantic component. To the extent that musical patterning is independent of the world of external possibilities that is the other, it pertains instead to the share of the self in the confrontation between the two. The force/resistance threshold where they meet, as represented in the unfolding of music, is less a window opening out onto the other, as it is in speech, than a mirror in which we rehearse and admire our own inventiveness and vitality. At the same time, all this elaboration of the preverbal and prerational layer of vocalizing amounts to a symbolic taming of our animal natures.

In singing, anatomy expands into temporality, because lungs and larynx take more time to realize their sonic potential as pitch and resonance than is required by the surface apparatus to articulate the phonemes of speech. And these depth-generated prolongations provide material for the long/short distinctions that are the rhythmic life of music.

An aphorism by Chazal states that "we speak with our lips to explain, with our throats to convince." Music can be convincing without benefit of explanations, even without the participation of human throats. Nothing in the practice of speaking corresponds to the use of musical instruments, and this can be related to music's commitment to a rhetoric of intonation rather than to a logic dependent on phonemic articulation. Notes are certainly easier to produce mechanically than vocables would be, but there is the even more basic point that speech has no need of instruments. Such devices as flutes and synthesizers expand the resources of music beyond what the voice can provide, but the examples of talking drums or whistle or computer speech, which can at best barely match the information-bearing capacity of the original, show what a marvel of efficiency the supralaryngeal vocal apparatus is.

On the other hand, the kind of sensuous enrichment music gains through the use of instruments is a side issue for words—unless the words are meant to be sung. There is surprisingly little wordless vocal music. Perhaps listeners find the sounds coming from a human throat unconvincing without the sort of explanation a song text provides; but instruments succeed in being convincing even without using words. If we think of instruments as alternatives to the voice, we must see them as playing a role equivalent not just to the pitch-generating laryngeal voice alone but to the singing voice as an entirety, text and all. This leads to the suspicion that instruments may sometimes serve musicians as a way to be acceptably speechless—sooner even an inarticulate singer than a talking bassoon—a way to be free of the clutter of verbally sustained images and attitudes and left to the devices of music alone.

PHYLOGENETICALLY WE get a prior/subsequent opposition for intonation and phonemic articulation, for a larynx capable of modulating pitch is found in all primates, and in many other orders as well (here is the seat of the force/resistance:self/other model for vocalization presented in Chapter 2), but phonemic articulation is dependent on the emergence in modern man of a new layer of interference with exhalation. This has a neurological component too. Functions specific to speech are handled largely independently from other sounds in the brain. It has long been known that the loss of the ability to speak does not necessarily involve any loss of the ability to sing, even to sing words, and stuttering typically does not carry over to singing. The unsurprising claim has been made that the speech centers of the brain are recent evolutionary developments: prior/subsequent again. Ontogenetically too intonation and phonemic articulation polarize according to the prior/subsequent scheme, for a newborn baby vocalizes to great effect in a prephonemic and presyntactic way.

Polyphony, like the use of instruments, is an option often exercised in both vocal and instrumental music—it is the dominant option in the modern European tradition—but is rarely found in conversation, except as the result of a miscalculation. This further asymmetry between the two activities may also be referable to music's primary commitment to resonant pitch play, the sort of thing the prephonemic larynx can do. The equipment specific to song is in place and in use months before the baby engages in any sustained and intricate self-and-other give-and-take.

At this earliest stage, developmental psychology assumes that the infant's awareness has the configuration I have described as the topology of Field 3, diffused in a kind of hologram in which there is no perceiver/perceived or knower/known distinction. The functions specific to speech (and thus to Field 2) including phonemic articulation are activated later, along with the gradual emergence in the young child of a sense of the self as an entity that is sustained in a reciprocal relationship with an other that has others in it. Speech is the prime vehicle of this dialogue.

If we suppose that music continues to make Field 3—the sense of self as world that is associated with prelinguistic vocalizing—available in adulthood, then we have a way of understanding the polyphonic option. By virtue of its very unstructuredness, this worldview can accommodate all sorts of structures while retaining its essential nondualistic nature: it can accommodate words (aphasics can remember the texts of songs, from which we can conclude that song texts are processed in the parts of the brain responsible for music, not speech); it can accommodate verbally defined individuals in a Lied or aria, or absorb them into a congregational hymn. Even the oppositional tautness of dialogue can be presented lyrically (though this is not one of music's strengths), usually in recitative, a genre that evolved specifically to accommodate ordinary speech. An operatic finale elevates the normally deplorable social situation in which everyone is talking at once far above the merely acceptable and makes it an occasion for aesthetic pleasure. (Ensemble singing can actually increase the intelligibility of words over what it would be if everyone concerned were speaking the lines in question, because the degree of control exercised in music over pitch and rhythm makes it possible to segregate different utterances each to a particular register, or rate of speed, or part of the measure, or all of these at once.)

Polyphony is an accommodation of diversity very different from the antiphonal negotiations between separate individuals that make up conversation. It seldom occurs to two conversationalists to say the same thing at the same time, and when they do they are embarrassed, or amused, or both. But musicians are always making a point of doing the same or carefully related things at the same time. In polyphony the individual ranges and timbres of the contributing voices and instruments submit to a single evolving image, and the participants' sense of autonomy shades over into a collective identity, that of the performing group and, in a more distanced and passive form, that of the temporary society of an audience. This may be seen as an elaborated continuation of the preverbal vocalizer's worldview.

I F W E move out in time from the level of the minimal features of
song and speech represented by intonation and phonemic articulation, the center/periphery opposition metamorphoses into cen-
tripetal/centrifugal. Once again notational practices are suggestive.

The modern European notation of music reflects a concern
with the exact management of relative duration according to an
array of fixed units related to each other by simple ratios. Their
flow is controlled by a background of steady pulses and groups of
pulses (measures). The experience of recurrence is centripetal in
the sense that it confirms what we already have. Repetition is never
experienced as being literal, because each new recurrence has a
different history from the previous ones; nevertheless the experience is one of movement in place. Verbal notation, on the other
hand, shows no more concern for relative duration than it does for
pitch (making an exception for the arrangement into lines and
stanzas of verse).

The song by Purcell cited at the beginning shows this
centripetal tendency of music at work in other dimensions as well
(see Appendix). One set of pitches is drawn upon throughout; series
of intervals recur analogously. A prominent example is the four-
note figure that opens the accompaniment. No measure of the song
is without some version of this figure, stated on one pitch level or
another. It forms part, in turn, of a three-measure ostinato that has
a grip on the entire song. And in its largest dimension the song
doubles back on itself, closing with a repetition of the opening
section. Although not all songs are as self-enfolded as this one,
most would make the point that music's reasoning is essentially
circular.

One kind of verbal discourse does double back on itself,

and one word for it, "verse," is derived indirectly from the Latin "vertere," "to turn." The turnings of verse are often synchronized in song with those of music, as can be seen in Purcell's piece by comparing his phrases with Dryden's lines.

There are other sorts of centripetal inward turning in poetry that tend to a merging of particulars into the whole. Metaphor, for example, encourages the reader to achieve a stereoptical fusion of images in terms of some unspecified common focus. And each rhyme is the copula in a metaphor which in generalized form states: there is a realm in which the diverse things we are talking about come together and fuse, and a common resonance can stand for that place. The structural parallelism of a series of stanzas carries this effect over into larger dimensions, and a strophic musical setting of those stanzas reinforces the effect. Music is free to take all of this further, because it is free of the need to make discursive sense, and it can drag verse along with it, as we see in Purcell's repetitions of "music," "wond'ring," and so forth, repetitions that had no place in Dryden's poem.

It is the Latin "prorsus," meaning "straight on," that underlies the word "prose." Prose and everyday speech are engaged in the serious practical business of keeping up with events, or better still of getting ahead of them, and repeating words or phrases in conversation always has something ignominious about it. When one person echoes what someone else has just said, the intent seems to be either servile or mocking. Even in those cases in which remarks are repeated only because they were not understood the first time, the repetition is accompanied by an exasperated sense of interrupted flow. Triviality is the impression produced by rhymes and parallel constructions in prose and casual talk alike, both of which normally seek or even indulge in a looseness and unpredictability of unfolding. Someplace Trotsky wrote that the rhythm of prose is like that of a shutter banging in the wind. Like conversation, prose must be left unfastened to anything like meter because it is far more circumstantial in its orientation than is verse, responding to the irregular internal flow of ideas and the chancy external flow of events.

Taken singly, words give us more to think about than individual notes do. The word "music" has each listener thinking different but probably related things, in every case directing attention far out beyond the resonances of the syllables themselves. And because those resonances have an only arbitrary connection with the object they direct attention to, more than one configuration of sounds could do essentially the same trick. By contrast there are no synonyms or paraphrases in music itself, as those terms are ordinarily applied to speech. No note in a musical passage could be replaced with another without altering the entire effect of the passage.

The preceding chapter argued that speech in general has a centrifugal thrust that dilates the shared present of speakers and has them taking their bearings by what once purportedly was the case, or what is the case (according to someone) but someplace else, or what they hope or fear may or may not eventually happen. To the extent they are committed to speech, people view their lives as unfolding at the focus of circumstances beyond the reach of the senses. It is because speech takes the participants in a conversation where the senses cannot follow to provide confirmation for what is said that lying is such an easily accessible resource. But since music is not essentially in the business of representing things beyond itself, it follows that it cannot misrepresent them either.

All reading of signs has to begin where all perception does, in a process of adaptation to a physical signal, a process that might be called protosemiotic. In the cases both of music and of speech this involves moving along with a sound signal that unfolds in time and integrating its various time-span layers: note, phrase, and so on in the case of music; phoneme, word, sentence in speech.

Speech treats this stage primarily as a means to further significances. Further significances can emerge from musical discourse as well, but the center of the musical experience remains the protosemiotic transaction itself, framed by style and genre and the particular social worlds and occasions they imply. Music is a dualistic trick for suspending duality: participants do form a duality of self and other with the music they perform or listen to, but to attend deeply to this other is to merge with it. To whatever extent music does not point to a world beyond the cognitive and motor activity of constituting it out of the raw material of sound, it gives the participants a sense of themselves as individuals with a central responsibility for the creation of their own provisional worlds; such fellow-inhabitants of that world as composer and performer or fellow-performer are not vividly present as individuals. In any of these roles the participants are released for the duration of the performance from dependence on some outer, oppositional world. At its most fulfilled, the world the participants synthesize is a self-validating, nondualistic world of presence in, and through movement.

This may help to explain another asymmetry between speech and music, the social acceptability of humming to oneself as opposed to the unacceptability of talking to oneself. Rooted in an acknowledgment of otherness and others, speech is essentially dialogical, so that talking to oneself is publicly and absurdly a matter of engaging with phantoms. But since the basic materials of

music, pitches and durations, contain no direct reference to a surrounding world, music has about it a self-sufficiency that can either take or leave the interlocutor.

But Purcell's song sets a text that *is* explicitly about something outside itself. If "Music for a while" is taken to be a view of
music, where is its viewing point? Whose voice is describing and
demonstrating in it the power of song? This is the sort of question
searchingly treated by Edward T. Cone in his book *The Composer's
Voice.* Is this Dryden's voice, or perhaps that of the character in
Dryden's play? Purcell's? The present performer's, or that of the
original singer in 1692? The listener's voice?

Perhaps the answer is: in varying degrees several or even all
of these at once. But in the best realized performances of the best
realized works still another voice dominates all of these, a voice
without a viewpoint. It does not speak from one location to a hearer
in another. Rather than acknowledging and negotiating differences
between the perspectives of speaker and listener it sings their commonality. Perhaps the voice of nondualistic presence is a prein-
dividuated voice without a history, a voice too deep and too ancient
to have a name. The text is there, as T. S. Eliot once said of the
words of a poem, partly to keep those parts of the mind and body
responsible for words engaged while the song goes about its deeper
work.

T H I S   C H A P T E R sets out a contrastive ordering of some traits
of singing and speaking, beginning with the anatomical sites that
have most to do with defining their most distinctive characteristics, the larynx and the mouth. These are interpreted as expressing
a contrast between center and periphery. Then their ontogeny and
phylogeny are analyzed as polarizing around a prior/subsequent

distinction, and their psychological orientation as exemplifying an opposition between centripetal and centrifugal. This view of song is seen as applying to most instrumental music as well, which is taken to be the displacement of pitch manipulation to new sites outside the body.

In conclusion, I would like to suggest that this last opposition, centripetal/centrifugal, points to a functional interdependency of speech and music, based on a claim that the metasensory expansiveness of speech creates a need in speakers (a need that will vary greatly from individual to individual) for a range of compensatory activity. Music—along with ritual and the other arts—is centripetal because speech is centrifugal. The differentiation of vocal sound at the body's periphery that yields the phonemes of speech, and so supports Field 2, brings with it a sense of the center as something that is determined by its shifting periphery, of self as a function of other. Speakers extend and elaborate, in the form of music, a more primitive layer of sounding than that distinctively involved with speech in order to counterbalance the tendencies to hyperextension in the dominant adaptive modality. Whereas conversation and written prose are rooted in the separateness of their participants within a world of common concerns and shared values and moves toward reconciling them, music faces the other way, beginning in an assumed central oneness which it then articulates, sometimes in highly elaborate ways. It can draw into itself tokens of differentiated real-world experience, such as observations about music's powers of beguilement.

Music is about the centering of awareness. The more centered awareness is, the more everything in awareness becomes a function or an aspect of the center. And music centers awareness in an object with no sharply defined utilitarian location in the world:

the more centered awareness is in such an object, the more does that object come to be provisionally identified with the totality of the world, and the less is the other a consideration. When this is carried still further, everything becomes center, and this is the defining condition for Field 3.

As the talking animal, we talk ourselves out of innocence, the primitive sense of being unconditionally here, and right, the source from which the world takes any meaning it has. But we can sing our way back into innocence again, restoring a sense of balance by asserting the authenticity of our sheer self-sufficient presence in the world. Insofar as we are musicians we are to a far greater extent centered in the synthetic sensuous actuality of the moment than we are as speakers, caught up in a world that is a function of our own synthesizing presence at its center and relatively innocent of real-life concerns and circumstances. Purcell's setting of the word "music" does not cancel its referential significance but does dim it in favor of involving us in an immediate process in which the dominant concern is a self-referring nexus of pitches and durations. All language must be allowed its considerable measure of self-reference—the point is central to some of the most vigorous recent literary criticism. But in the case of practical discourse such self-reference is like the mutual involvement of the two blades of a pair of scissors, whose interaction translates ultimately into making a difference beyond them both.

It might seem contradictory that the assertion of a great simplicity, our presence in the world, should assume such complex forms as songs by Purcell, to say nothing of the *Vespers of 1610* or *Moses and Aaron*. But even innocence needs an occasion, an object capable of focusing it. The mediating animal seeks this quality of vibrant immediacy through the mediacy of works of art because taking charge by proxy, by means of tools or representations, is built into the human strategy for survival.

And then, a complex mind is not fully addressed and engaged by simplicity. Complexity brings with it the enticement of a challenge to our painfully acquired powers of perceptual synthesis and control, and the promise of the excitement of successfully overcoming the challenge. Music has evolved its kinds of complexity—complexities in the management of pitch, timbre, rhythm, form—in keeping up with the complexities of the world that speech orders and represents. Words represent the articulations of this world, and music mimics the referential articulations of words with a nonreferential articulatedness that neutralizes the centifugal force of linguistic awareness. If music gives us innocence, it is a synthetic innocence—informed, crafty, and ripe.

Significantly absent from absorption in a song is a sense of otherness populated by others, an out-there oppositional world waiting for people to do something about it, or perhaps not waiting before it does something about them. Each new development in a piece of music comes from within it and must be attended to. It represents a choice made in the interests of the whole occasion, and its effect is not to add something on at the end of what has come before but to differentiate and expand the special resonance of the whole.

As this process continues, past and future are to a degree disalienated from the present. If the past has built up a consistent pattern for the timing of the beat, for example, this is interpreted as the possibility of predicting the timing of its recurrences, so that this much of the future is an attenuated part of the present. There are other larger and freer units that may recur and can be anticipated, from figure and phrase on up to section. Pieces and whole musical styles differ greatly in the degree to which they make use of repetition, but on one level or another it is a widespread resource: music's self-enfolded aspect comes from these fixities of movement, these quasi-presents on many levels of integration.

Repetition helps the participants collaborate with the progress of the piece, sometimes so deeply they may feel that they and the piece are two aspects of one process. For listeners to move along with a regular and so predictable beat, for example, is for them to be, in a limited sense, the same as something that reaches them from the outside and so to weaken the sense of any distinction between within and without, self and other. For the time being they feel continuous with whatever matters. Contingent on the continuation of the music, they sustain the healing illusion of their noncontingent presence at that center which is everywhere.

Chapter Five

WORDS IN MUSIC

T H E   R E C I T A T I O N tones of plainsong, recitatives and arias, Sprechgesang, talking blues and melodrama: these are some of the forms of accommodation reached in the West by the two major ranges of sounding thought, speech and music.

One theory about the relationship between the two is implied in Beaumarchais's "if it's too silly to say, you can sing it"; Rameau is reported to have been willing to set *La Gazette de Hollande* to music, with Rossini similarly disposed toward laundry lists.

Addison took this further when he wrote that "nothing is capable of being well set to music that is not nonsense." Presumably this is an ironically playful way of saying that a great deal of what is set to music is in fact nonsense, when judged as literature. Addison's comment might have been motivated by irritation over the failure of an opera for which he had written the libretto, *Rosamund* (1707); however well or ill that particular libretto was set to music, Addison is not likely to have thought of it as nonsense.

Certainly music is a great leveler of literary distinctions, and serious poets have seldom put themselves deliberately in the path of musical setting (the apprehensiveness is almost tangible in Goethe's remark that "the effect produced by music is so powerful that it dominates everything"). On the other hand, composers will just as rarely make a point of seeking out nonsense as the starting point for their songs. There are limits on what most of them will set, but the limits do not consist of a ceiling on literary quality; in fact, the musical impulse is often fired by a brilliant poem. Yet musical settings of great verse say more about composers' tastes in literature (in some cases still more about their vanity in wanting to be associated only with the best) than they do about how good a text must be from a literary standpoint to produce a good song.

But there is no redemption by association for weak composers: "noble words never saved a bad tune, whereas a good tune has often rescued ignoble words" (Fox Strangways does not say that the good tune would not do still better with good words). The rescue has its price, for whether ignoble or noble, the words, for better or for worse, lose in translation to song much of their original form and impact, often being distorted to a point that affects comprehensibility.

Certainly some verbal purposes are served by singing. There is a song literature of indoctrination and persuasion, illustrated by love songs and songs of worship, the sung playground taunts of children, vendors' street cries and auctioneers' chants and advertising jingles. Some messages achieve a kind of penetration of the listeners' defenses when sung and a perfusion of his awareness that speech alone cannot bring about. Much of our wariness is a verbal and analytical defense of the perimeter; music gets past this and can draw some words down with it into the center.

THE WAYS a given text might be spoken are innumerable; equally there is no limit to the number of ways it might be set to music, but a fundamental difference of import separates the two groups. Reading a text like Dryden's lyric from *Oedipus:*

> Musick for a while
> Shall your cares beguile:
> Wond'ring how your pains were eas'd:—
> And disdaining to be pleas'd;—
> Till *Alecto* free the dead
> > From their eternal bands;
> Till the snakes drop from her head,
> And whip from out her hands

could sound languorous, or even coolly detached, or assertive and insistent, depending on such things as the pitch contour and resonance and tempo of the speaker's delivery. These are like so many different ways of tinting an etching whose linear design remains the most important thing about it. Central to each of these readings is a thought about music's power, but in any singing of the same lines this thought loses its sharply focused quality to become diffused through a differently defined occasion, a particular quality of resonance.

Even in a spoken recitation that is accompanied by instrumental music, as in melodrama, there is some softening of the listeners' perception of crisply verbal junctures, and a rounding and filling out of their sense of the dimensions of what they are hearing. If the recitation were to be delivered in Sprechgesang, each syllable turning viscous and stretching almost beyond recognition, the effect would be even further removed from the everyday than if the text were sung to a tune, despite the use in tunes of a nonconversational kind of pitch and rhythm.

The simplest plainsong recitation formula is as radical a stylization of speech as either Sprechgesang or tune, but a stylization that moves in the opposed direction of restrictiveness. If Dryden's stanza were chanted to a lesson tone, essentially one note repeated for each syllable of text and inflected by cadential figures, the listener entering and moving with so radical a renunciation of variability would in the process renounce anything like an ordinary grip on reality and drift into a trancelike state of becalmed and dissociated awareness. Here the mind is like a still pond; a word of text here and there, or any other associated experiences, drops into it and diffuses through it.

Purcell's setting of these words (see Appendix) works very differently from any of these while still keeping the quality of resonant presence common to them all at its center.

There is none of the renunciation associated with a lesson tone about this: the process of adapting to its restlessly self-transforming flow of rhythmic, melodic, and harmonic developments is an actively kinetic experience for both performer and listener. Yet it is by no means extreme as an example of the musical expansion of text. The acoustic variables characteristic of music— pitch options extending through several octaves, for example, or prolongations over time of a single sound that challenge the sustaining capacity of the lungs, or a whole range of harmonic and textural possibilities—cover such a broad spectrum compared to the phonations that define speech on the level of sound, and are so elastic, that exercising the musical options on the verbal ones can distort a text past all recognition.

Dryden's lyric proceeds from its opening promise of musical beguilement to a fancifully learned close claiming that music's powers will hold sway until Alecto, "the unresting," shall, in effect, take her rest. In its shape, the verse progressively opens out from the two short rhyming lines at the start through the concluding quatrain of longer lines rhymed alternately. As a general rule, speech pushes on, music circles in place. Like music, verse has a tendency, in Coleridge's words, to double back, "over and over, on its own logic." But its movement is more pronouncedly helical than the relatively flat rotation of music, because it must accommodate the nature of its material and discourse is compulsively nonrepetitive.

Worldwide and over historical time the largest group of songs is organized strophically, the text proceeding, as to its content, additively, either cutting a succession of new facets into a central percept or drawing a narrative along its course, while at the same time the music moves in a closed ring of sound comprised of a repeating segment anywhere from a few notes long to the length of a stanza. "Music for a while" illustrates music's self-enfolded aspect differently, in ways pointed out in the previous chapter: the ubiquitous four-note figure, the ostinato, the doubling back at the end (not found, by the way, in the printed text of the play).

Purcell preserves little sense of the line as a metrical unit or of the relative metrical weight of different syllables within the line, as a schematic representation of his setting of the first two lines shows (see Appendix). From the rhythmic point of view, Purcell's composition decomposes Dryden's into a kind of impassioned speech afflicted with palilalia ("shall all, all, all, shall all, all, all, shall all") and adapted to musical meter. The result is a new entity guided on one level by Dryden's words, but very little by his verse, either in its prosodic aspect or in the unfolding of its imagery. Yet the resulting song is the kind of thing that could give misreading a good name, at least as perpetrated by musicians of genius.

A WORKING assumption common among writers on music is that every significant detail in a song is determined by its text and can be explained by it. The many cases of very different and equally acceptable songs that set the same poem make it obvious that the assumption could only hold in a broad and weak sense, but this has not loosened its grip on musicography.

A song that could be regarded as no more than a musical blow-up of its text would clearly have small intrinsically musical interest. Verse and music work very differently and a song is music only to the extent that it is musically determined and self-consistent and therefore independent of its text, however smoothly it may also mesh with the character of the words. The assumption that the music of a song exists to express its text is hard to reconcile with the fact that music almost always becomes the dominant factor in the merger of the two arts, and it encourages us to view songs the wrong way to. Analysis should deal with the text of a song in the spirit of archaeology, uncovering its remains embedded in the music while acknowledging its progenitive role.

The tension between the rival claims of words and music and the threat posed to text by music have produced a number of calls for the reform of text-setting in the course of the history of European music. One such episode was the indignation of the clerics at the Council of Trent over settings of sacred texts that obscured their meaning. More than once the focus has been opera (Gluck and Calzabigi in the third quarter of the eighteenth century, Wagner in the mid-nineteenth), and all these reformers consistently took the side of the qualities and values of the text. Somehow no Monteverdi ever stood up to say that music was being mauled and stifled by words, proclaiming a *seconda practica* to reassert its claims: music was always being viewed as the aggressor in an unequal contest in which words needed the help of still more words to defend their interests. In all this there is a hint that music is dangerously Dionysian and words the respectable side to be on. And in the end, the new works resulting from these reforms—the Monteverdi *stile concertato* madrigals, Wagner's music dramas— had a predominantly musical profile after all, as though the reform movements had been infiltrated by the opposition from the outset.

Certainly the assumption that everything depends on the text is a comfortable one to make. It piously allows each of the arts involved its dignity. Discussions of text are moreover easier to write and more entertaining to read than are analyses of music. The vocabulary we have for the elusive liquidities of music—modulation to the subdominant, German sixth chord, and the rest of it— presents even to those who understand it a cold and technical surface compared to the one offered by the rich texture of the language of literary criticism (the next chapter takes up the question of representing music in some detail). Dryden's imagery is appealing as a point of entry for the analyst, as it must originally have been for the composer himself—except that the analyst may not be as willing as the composer to go beyond that point. In the case of "Music" this would be particularly regrettable since Purcell, like all the great song writers, so radically transforms his material. Schoenberg may have been reacting polemically against the kind of exegesis that stops at "madrigalisms" and other superficialities when he wrote that in his experience detailed knowledge of a poem can actually hinder the appreciation of a song that sets it.

A good poem is expressively self-sufficient, a passionately and precisely calculated whole that stands or falls as a whole. The poem no longer exists if its vowels are distended and its rhythms broken: it is not only its comprehensibility but also its artistic shape that is affected by such distortions. However effective the text of Purcell's song, it is no longer Dryden's poem.

IT IS music that needs verse, not the other way around. In song after song, and the Purcell song is no exception, the composer might have modeled his approach to the poem he is setting on a kind of affectionate cannibalism in which the diner will retain from the meal certain of the victim's virtues after destroying his substance (this food-chain image could be extended: if music metabolizes verse, then it might be said that verse metabolizes words, which metabolize the world). Once the text has served its initial purpose it has been known to fade away entirely, leaving a purely instrumental piece behind or even yielding its place to a completely different text. There is more of Chopin's song "The Maiden's Wish" in Liszt's transcription for piano solo than there is in a recitation of its poem.

The appetite of music for words is reflected in the rarity of wordless song. As vocalizers we are for very practical reasons first of all speakers. Wordless vocal melodies are least problematic when the occasion, such as solitary humming, does not involve social communication, or goes beyond it, as in the case of Hassidic prayer. Otherwise singing without words we feel impotent and incomplete, as though deprived of the use of our hands.

This is in part physical: the syllable-making apparatus is there and wants to be used. We miss the sensuous feel of vocables, the bite and the taste they have in the mouth and their power to articulate and shape rhythms. To a great extent the composer in pursuit of texts is looking for occasions for resonance (this may explain the appearance of the word "all," with its resonant open "a," in the second phrase of Purcell's song, even though it is not present in Dryden's text). Scat singing and other vocalizing to nonsense syllables take care of this range even as they suspend the range of imagery found in ordinary texts, but imagery addresses another part of the apparatus that wants to be used. In giving play to the major range of thought, the words of a song locate the music in relation to it and bring about a provisional integration of the two.

Yet often what is said seems not to matter very much. How much thought does the average listener to Purcell's song give to Alecto, her snakes, and her whip? The presence in this lyric setting of one of the Furies seems positively unhelpful until we notice that the song was originally used in *Oedipus* to raise and placate the dead Lajus "and those who were murdered with him." But once the text is present, good enunciation on the part of the singer should cause it to be as clearly present as possible, for the listener stands to gain nothing either musically or verbally from struggling in vain to understand what is being said.

Because only so much attention is available for either a poem or a song, and the musical setting of a poem cuts severely into the amount that can be separately allocated to it as a literary object, the texts chosen by composers tend to favor vividness over intricacy, with states of overwhelmedness in several varieties first in preference: love, grief, exuberance, awe. A little after these comes foolishness. One thing that is hard to find outside of recitative is casual, sensible talk.

Whatever the power of music to rescue ignoble words and dominate everything, composers have not often deliberately tested it, and despite the statements of Rameau and Rossini, there is little in the way of newspaper stories or laundry lists in the song literature, though Milhaud's settings of excerpts from catalogs of flowers and agricultural machinery deserve mention. Perhaps composers prefer verse to prose because the incantatory quality they are after is already present in a poem; the challenge then is to construct something comparable by demolishing the poem as poem and absorbing what remains—certain words in a certain order—in a new affectively centering structure.

WHATEVER ITS explanatory power for modern European song, this model of songwriting as logophagia has presumably not applied always and everywhere. At some dawn of song, and continuing to the present day in some traditions, the line of verse and the musical phrase were the same structure, and the words were born along with the music or in some cases followed after, shaping themselves to preexistent musical formulas. According to this view, the acts of appropriation on the part of composers that are known as songwriting are the latter-day result of a split between "poetry" and "music" that has seen these two go their own increasingly complex and specialized ways.

A practical result has been the emergence of a new genre. Words for music are no more violated by musical setting than are shoes by wearing, since neither shoes nor librettos have a higher reason for existing. Librettists and song lyricists, the specialists in this genre, must have some of the instincts of cartoonists: a sense of the psychologically vivid and elemental and a willingness to let subtlety go (except that an inability to do otherwise serves just as well). They must write with an ear for melodies yet unheard—as both Metastasio and Wagner testified they did—providing them with a strong focus and leaving them plenty of room.

Which of its tributaries, words or music, dominates in a song depends finally on which of the two a listener is more interested in. But listeners tend to favor the music.

If, as claimed in the last chapter, the underlying objective of music is to compensate for the centrifugal orientation that accompanies verbal activity, then logically it would be counterproductive to pay the kind of attention to the words of a song that is appropriate to words in their everyday uses. Of course there are circumstances, of a political nature for example, that might largely block out the music setting a highly charged text. Or a fresh text might stand out against the background of an overfamiliar tune or one that manipulates tired formulas in an unenterprising way.

The acoustic and perceptual odds do favor the music: singing distorts the sounds of words as to both their enunciation and their duration relative to one another and goes on to compete with the distorted result. The full resonance cultivated in some styles of singing tends to overwhelm delicate consonants. Prolongation of vowel sounds, repetition of certain words and phrases, the introduction of rests all may stretch the normal time span for taking in a sentence past the breaking point. Meanwhile the music is making multiple cognitive demands of its own on attention in the sectors of pitch, timbre, amplitude, and duration, over several simultaneously unfolding time spans: rhythm, phrase, section, piece—the song text interferes with none of this.

If attention takes the path of lesser cognitive resistance, it will favor the music over the words for these reasons alone; but there is another. Taking in music involves one cognitive operation less than does understanding speech (just as singing a note without text involves one less *physical* operation than saying a syllable), because music largely dispenses with the semantic component that is speech's reason for being. Musical significance doesn't depend, as verbal does, on a lexicon of referents, and consequently perceiving music is not the uninterrupted process of instant translation from sound to sense that understanding speech is: even granting the importance of socialization to full participation in particular musical traditions, the fact remains that living the sound itself, in all its sectors and over all its time spans, is the root of its musical meaning. This is what was referred to in the last chapter as protosemiosis.

This protosemiosis is less ambiguous, event for event, than is the semiosis of speech. The sound of a word is as clearly what it is as is the sound of a note—but that is only the beginning, for words not only have denotations but in many cases alternate denotations from among which a choice has to be made, and a further range of connotations, altogether a far richer associational network than the one constituted by, say, common practice harmony. This is one way to understand Mendelssohn's famous remark: "What the music I love expresses to me, is not thought too *indefinite* to be put into words, but, on the contrary, too *definite.*" One aspect of music's edge over words in the competition between them for the attention of a listener to a song is its relative trustworthiness.

T E X T A N D music converge on an objective that is not completely identifiable with either one, a sense in performers and listeners of a centered fullness of presence detached from the give and take of the everyday. By the nature of its materials music comes closer to this objective than words do, as much for what it lacks in associations extending beyond the moment as for what it contributes in a positive way; but a flow of present awareness is more profoundly centered still in a dancer's body and so it is that dance absorbs the music that is heard with it.

The changing patterns of pressure and density in Purcell's progress through his closed world of sounds and Dryden's images of pain beguiled flow together and are held in a standing wave of vital presence whose modulations of contour, mass, and color do not affect the essential stillness of its movement. As with the experience of sound itself, there is no foreground awareness of inside and outside in a good performance of "Music," or of here and there. Performer and listener and setting are all felt as external and incidental aspects of an incantatory resonance, a sense of vibrant swelling stillness that brings its participants a conviction of their unconditional presence in the world.

Chapter Six

WORDS ON MUSIC

LISTENING TO the ringing of a bell is moving inwardly to an outward activity. The sound can't be heard for once and for all, as the bell itself might be seen, for it is never the same from instant to instant, the intensity of a listener's participation peaking with each stroke and dying back tremulously as the reverberations fade (other layers of response may comment on this basal layer by anticipating or highlighting or downplaying certain of its features).

Though listeners may know that these sensations originate in a clearly delimited and located object, the bell over there, still the actual sensations of adapting the flow of their attention to the ringing don't feel attached to that source, nor are the sensations restricted, as a ringing in the ears would be, to the other end of the transaction, to the inside of their heads. The sensations seem instead to be going on all around and through those who are listening.

Shifting attention from the sound to the word "ringing" brings with it a radical shift in the quality of awareness. The word alerts its hearers or readers to something not necessarily present here and now together with the word. The concept "ringing" is something itself quite still and enduring, despite the transitory sound of the word itself and the mobility of what it refers to. For all the variability among all the imaginable ringings to which it might direct attention, it is a figure clearly located as a foreground outlined against an implied background, the concept "silence," but at the same time available for combining with other such figures. In fact, it has more in common with other such figures, such as the concept "bell," than with actual ringing; we might even say that it has—just as regards its conceptually localized stability—more in common with the physical bell itself than with the ringing it refers to.

The gap between experience and representation in the case of the ringing of a bell can serve as a paradigm for what is involved in representing music. "How then does language manage, when it must interpret music? Alas, badly—very badly, it seems." Thus Roland Barthes; the resistance of music to representation has often been noted. The point isn't simply that music slips through the net of language—for what, after all, does not, to one degree or another?—but there can be few gaps between an experience and its representation wider than the one between music and its analyses and descriptions. I propose to exploit it in a theoretical way in this chapter by using it to bring out some features both of representation in general and of music in particular; perhaps the very distance between the two correspondingly enlarges the potential contribution each can make to a negative definition of the other.

The gap is especially striking because words and music are

such close neighbors physiologically and perceptually—if we stick
to spoken words and music in performance. And both take time.
But whereas the words that flow through music in song are, according to the argument of the preceding chapter, to a degree dissolved
in it, the discourses that flow over and around it, describing, ana-
lyzing, and evaluating, keep their distance. They are not isomor-
phic with the object they represent, nor do they typically run
concurrently with it. In order to give my discussion of words on
music some context, I will open the subject out to include representations of music in nonverbal media as well, so that the larger
subject of this chapter is the metamorphoses of aspect and import
that musical events undergo when they are represented in media
other than their native one. Their native medium is here considered to be sound; "music" is here understood to refer to "music in
performance," the ongoing involvement of performers and listeners
with an auditory occasion designed for the purpose.

There is a whole spectrum of representations of music to
consider, running all the way from scores to verbal explanations
and commentary and taking in verbal and gestural descriptions and
analyses both verbal and graphic along the way (electromechanical
representations—tapes and disks of various kinds—are not considered here, because with them the essential operations of encoding
and interpreting are a matter of machines talking to machines).
These various representations differ from each other most essentially in their differing kinds and degrees of correspondence to the
nature and detail of the pieces they represent. As different from
each other as are the extremes of the spectrum represented by a
score and a verbal analysis, they all have much in common besides
the particular pieces of music on which they may both focus. No
score, for example, is value free, any more than an analysis is: it

embodies judgments about the relative value of elements in the music in what its author has chosen to represent in it and what to leave out.

The broad objective behind all representing—not just the representing of music—is appropriation for new purposes, and such appropriation will necessarily involve denaturing and transforming the original in the process, assimilating it to some sign system under the representor's control, such as a language. Anything of any human interest or relevance at all will be picked up, at least by language, but, generally speaking, objects that most urgently need representing are those that in their original state are too vast, or too vague, fleeting, threatening, or inaccessible—or any combination of these—to be satisfactorily possessed and dealt with directly. Representation of such objects lends them such virtues as accessibility, permanence, or harmlessness as may be characteristic of some medium not their own, with the obvious drawback—or in some cases advantage—of sacrificing their impact in their own original terms. Though there is no general rule that representations are the more useful the greater their difference from their originals, there does seem to be some correlation between utility and difference. In any case representation puts things within our grasp, it makes them vicariously controllable and possessable. Any noun thus makes a good prototype representation; classic examples of more complex and substantial representations include fetishes, scapegoats (the indirect power the user of a token has over its original is an old topic in ethnography), and transitional objects.

IT WOULD be a mistake to proceed as though all representations of music were alike, and the next few paragraphs set out some of the ways in which they differ. First of all, they differ in their purposes; this will be taken up later. Next, they vary widely in what they treat as the object to be represented and in the detail with which they represent it. Philosophy, for example, typically represents music as being "all of music," and devotes little close analysis to particular performances. Ethnomusicology takes music to be inseparable from its contexts and may deal with representations of both performance and context in fine detail. A musicologist specialized in European music of privilege might devote a chapter to a history of style over the course of a century, or give the same amount of attention to one contredanse.

Since virtually all representations are reductive, it is important to be aware of just what is being reduced in them, and by how much. Such gestural representations as conducting or eurhythmics engage principally with the rhythmic range of music, while picking up on amplitude as well, but deal fitfully and arbitrarily with melodic, harmonic, and timbral detail. Visual representations can be the most detailed, as witness scores, but the point of an analytic diagram may depend on its suppression of irrelevant detail. Examples of more encompassing visual depictions might be Jules Chéret's painting of a figure standing for "La Musique" (1891), Stravinsky's drawing meant to show the style of his own "recent music," or Hindu raga-mala paintings.

A representation might be concerned exclusively with the auditory dimension of a performance, as a score is, or it might deal with the inner psychological states associated with participation in it, or it might do both. Verbal accounts tend to range more widely over both than any other form of representation. The gestures of a conductor do convey attitude; but in part because subjective states are not spatially delimited and stable, their depiction is famously difficult to bring off. Take Elaine Scarry on pain: "For the person in pain, so incontestably and unnegotiably present is it that 'having pain' may come to be thought of as the most vibrant example of what it is to 'have certainty,' while for the other person it is so elusive that 'hearing about pain' may exist as the primary model of what it is 'to have doubt.' Thus pain comes unsharably into our midst as at once that which cannot be denied and that which cannot be confirmed."

Yet in the case of the musical experience, the observation made above about the subjective states associated with it—that they are not spatially delimited and stable—applies just as well to its auditory dimension. The detail of a modern score does not mislead us into supposing that the nature of musical sound—its ephemerality, its ubiquity—is accurately conveyed there. So another variable among representations is their degree of iconicity or literalness with respect to the original.

Only a representation involving the same sense modality as the original could be truly iconic (for music, gesture comes the closest of the nonauditory ones). The auditory representation of music has not been found widely useful: most of its representations switch mode (an exception that comes to mind is Hans Keller's wordless and diagramless analyses). It might be objected that representations of music in speech—the most widely employed of all—use the same sensory channel that music does; but the configuration of speech sounds as phonemes with assigned significances entails a radically different mode of communication from that of music.

Representations often take a step beyond selective treatment of the original to rearrangement: analyses in particular treat the original order of the musical events they single out with great freedom. Each step away from the original state of the object is a step toward original creation (a model for this might be such structures as the Cathedral in Syracuse, Sicily, a seventh-century reformulation of the ruins of an earlier temple dedicated to Athena).

It is not only the object that is treated selectively in a representation but the medium of representation itself as well. Scores, for example, traditionally make little use of color or depth perspective. They do operate with spatial analogs, as in the case of the "high/low" convention for pitch, or the stylized depiction of a keyboard or fingerboard in a tablature. On the other hand, space rarely conveys rhythm, except in the crude respect that continuity of direction will indicate succession; conventional signs are the rule for rhythm but may also be used for pitch (in the cases of alphabetical notation and shape notes).

Finally, is the author of the representation present along with the work? Typically not; but some representations are themselves live performances, like a conversational account of a musical event. A conductor's performance is an example of a representation unfolding in the same time frame as its object.

JUST WHAT is the nature of the gap between music and representation? Representations—including verbal ones—tend strongly toward fixity and concentrated spatial localization. Vision is the prototype of understanding: we say in English "I see" and "I get the picture" as ways of saying "I understand" (though a possibly still deeper-rooted model is the prehensile "grasping" of an idea—which would still need to be fixed and localized to be graspable). The ideal visual object is stable and submits to our scrutiny (or grasp) for as long or as short a time as we choose.

There can be few human activities less conformable than

music to grasping and scrutinizing. The physical nature of sound—invisible oscillations diffusing through the atmosphere—is part of the problem. Another is the notorious difficulty of grasping the "flow of time." Music is like an ongoing experiment in pushing change as far as it can coherently be taken; by its very nature it challenges and frustrates the need to place things, fix and locate them—as for that matter does all motion, like that of an arrow in flight. The locus classicus for this problem is Zeno's third paradox of motion, in which the flight of an arrow shows up in analysis as a jerky chain of discrete locations, each of which stops time at some wholly ideal point.

Reification is also at work in music itself, if not to the degree to which it is found in graphic and verbal texts. If all art aspires to the state of music, as Pater claimed, then we might say that music returns the compliment by aspiring in a limited way to the state of architecture. Fixed rates of oscillation are reified as stable pitches, series of notes as phrases, and so on up to the repeatable—though not strictly fixed—itinerary called a piece. Still there is a considerable distance separating the direct perceptual experience of a fixed rate of change, say 440Hz, from that of fastening onto a concept such as "A," or a grapheme in the second space of the G clef.

The gap between fixity and flow that is built into the whole enterprise of representing music yields something like an inverse relationship in such representations between the degree of detail included and the degree to which the temporal quality of the original can be conveyed—except for gesture, no means of representation has the temporal agility of sound. Small wonder, in any case, that so much discussion in the field of music actually centers on music's verbal and physical support system: on scores and instruments, on the texts of songs and the plots of operas, on theoretical treatises, all of which sit with more docility for their portraits than do musical performances (accounts of verbal statements typically don't deal with their sound as such).

Scores can be gone through from start to finish (from left to right) as recipes for performances either real or imaginary, but the most remarkable thing about them is that they needn't be used this way. They can instead be the means to their users' detaching themselves from the sequence of events in the original and their rate of occurrence there and to constructing instead new entities—analyses—out of its materials. It is the stability of a visual object that allows a viewer this initiative and control over what it represents. By means of a score, a representation of anything in a piece can easily be lifted out of context and scrutinized for a length of time that has nothing to do with the time it takes to perform, and it can be confronted with passages widely separated from it (including passages from other pieces). Passages can be considered in any order; in fact, the whole thing can be run backward and/or upside down, if that is the score user's pleasure. While any of this is theoretically feasible without reference to a score, the score makes it all relatively effortless and so constitutes practically an incitement to analysis and judgment, which profit from the possibilities for scrutiny at leisure it provides; a performance, by contrast, moves the participant through its own sequence of events at its own pace.

Two chapters back I wrote of Purcell's song "Music for a while":

A prominent example [of a pattern recurring in the course of the piece] is the four-note figure that opens the accompaniment. No measure of the song is without some version of this figure, stated on one pitch level or another. And it forms part, in turn, of a three-measure ostinato that has a grip on the whole song. In its largest dimension the song doubles back on itself, closing with a repetition of the opening figure.

Only out of courtesy, or out of habit, or out of necessity perhaps, do we accept such descriptions as having anything to do with the vital activity of music making we enter into as listeners and performers. The score may be yet more dead, but is at least rich in the sort of detail captured by a photograph. Our courtesy in both these cases is like that we extend to a verbal account or a snapshot of a busy scene on a downtown street, except that in the case of music we are not concerned with pedestrians, cars, the street itself, but only with the busyness in all its particularity.

Of course no attempt was made in those comments on Purcell to reproduce the original. Verbal discourse about music breaks up the flow of musical sound into a series of eddies—not necessarily coterminous with such musical eddies as notes and phrases—each eddy a word, together with the concept that it labels, each a stoppage of the flow. The paragraph above is the record of one observer's isolation of a few such fixings—"figure," "accompaniment," "measure," "pitch," "ostinato"—from the stream of the piece, together with some comparisons made among them. These fixings emerge from the stable residue of memory and from study of the score, in other words more from a viewing point pulled back from the progress of the music than from a listening point within it.

These fixings conform to categories already in existence

and labeled before the observer encountered the piece, and by
means of their labels they can consort in sentences with anything
else that has a name. A lexicon makes the world that descends to us
from the past available, decomposed into stable bits, for the always
ongoing process of its reformulation.

In and of itself, discourse about music more closely resembles discourse about street scenes, stratospheric pollution, mush-
room gathering, or anything else at all than it does music itself (and
the notation of a melody is more like similar graphic displays,
showing perhaps the range of temperatures over the year, than like
the sound of the melody). The deaf are barred from full participation in music but not from joining the rest of us in verbalizing
about it.

Verbalizing confronts the multiplicity of the world with a
single broad process for assimilating it that includes many subject-
specific discourses. Each of these discourses responds to the general need—the chronically unanswerable metaquestion mentioned
in Chapter 3—to capture everything that matters, music, mush-
rooms, and the rest, for that major range of sociability which is
based upon the words that circulate among the members of a
language community.

The community is situated in what I have been calling
Field 2, a zone opened out, by words, around the here and now to
include history and the future and elsewhere, an aurally embodied
shifting panorama detached from the immediate input of the
senses. And so the object of any discourse must be denatured and
translated into terms transportable out of the object's own proper
time and place, so that it can be in a sense available in its own
absence (and being written, the brief account of the Purcell song
given above is received by the reader in the absence not only of the

object but of its original viewer as well, who is also absent from this account of his absence.)

A SCORE resembles a dried cod in preserving its original in a form suitable for storage and transport; the appropriate treatment restores both fish and music to consumable form when needed. Though representations are necessarily distortions and dilutions of their originals (the Hebrew poet Bialik compared reading a translation to kissing through a handkerchief) they are justified by the practical good they do. This is obvious in the case of a score (if not a handkerchief) but descriptions and analyses are useful too, if only because they enrich verbal and graphic thinking with a musical dimension. And the word can guide the ear: music is rarely taught by example alone. The distortions in an analysis or description can be constructive in complementing the distortions produced by naive listening and in emphasizing what the untrained ear misses.

I would like to suggest that another motive for representing music exists alongside the practical one, a need in most people some of the time to establish control over the things that matter deeply to them by converting them into alternate forms on which they place a personal stamp.

Sound has a side that is intrusive, uncontrollable, fearful: it is perfusive, invasive, peremptory; it goes off into a dimension all its own in its detachment from the enduring, spatially defined aspect of the world (Nietzsche wrote of the ear as the organ of fear). An article by Kohut and Levarie suggests that music represents an attempt to establish control over the fearful side of sound. But music has its own fearful side: it can induce feelings of overwhelmedness and ecstasy and states of dissociation that may shade over into trance. There is a degree of surrender of control and individuality in all this, an effect that can be at once disturbing and disturbingly difficult to describe; Freud wrote frankly about it:

> [I have spent long periods of time with works of art] trying to apprehend them in my own way, i.e. to explain to myself what their effect is due to. Whenever I cannot do this, as for example with music, I am almost incapable of obtaining any pleasure. Some rationalistic, or perhaps analytic, turn of mind in me rebels against being moved by a thing without knowing why I am thus affected, and what it is that thus affects me.

It may be that in the case of music it is just what makes the object in both its acoustic and its psychological ranges hard to represent isomorphically—which is to say its invisibly ubiquitous and radically temporal nature—that gives a special edge to the need to establish the kind of control over it that representation provides. But truth to the nature of the original needn't be an objective of representation. In fact it seems that, as in the case of representations made for practical purposes, it is to a degree their very distance from the original that gives those motivated by a need for psychological control their utility.

To begin with, transcribers responsible for a score or authors of a description or analysis wrest the psychological initiative from the music: *they* are now doing something to *it*. In the visual domain we speak of "capturing a likeness." Then, they achieve a retreat from intimacy with it by shifting the scene of their encounter with it to a (probably) nonauditory one under their own control. Nietzsche wrote that jokes are the epitaphs of emotions, but analyses serve even better: we might note that nothing is a more effective epitaph for a joke than a good analysis of it. And since the representor has in some sense duplicated the original creator's achievement, he attains to a kind of peer status with him—or even to a stance of superiority, if the representation is capped with a judgment (and this may apply to a judgment that is approving as well as to a disapproving one). (Benjamin Boretz has pointed out the danger in all this to our sense of music: "Sound can also annihilate sound; conversation can also annihilate its antecedent experience; thought can be an anechoic chamber for its objects; discourse can remove us from the scene of our attention altogether.")

There are further consolations of objectivity. To the extent the new setting is in some widely accessible medium, say a natural language, then the act of representation is like falling in step with a crowd, exchanging the singularity and vulnerability of private response in the grip of the instant for an enduring, publicly testable would-be verity. Perhaps the analyst will assimilate the work to some a priori analytical language or paradigm—such as semiotics or communications theory or Schenkerian analysis—and in so doing claim it for some academically select society: such communities depend for their survival on a continuing flow of acquisitions.

Given the multiplicity of discourses humans maintain, it is inevitable that music undergo a wide range of metamorphoses, that like anything else that matters it be subject to an unending process of representation in a variety of domains. The defensive motive is proposed as only one among several for this process. And of course we can both eat our musical cake, participatively, and have it, in represented form, although the success of a musical experience probably depends on keeping some part of awareness unencumbered by graphic instructions and free of verbal perspectives.

ONE CAN imagine a way of dealing with music that would come much closer than the usual analysis to its nature in performance, by acknowledging its momentousness. It would focus on the present, perhaps on a series of presents lifted from the piece under analysis. Its most basic difference from the usual approaches would be its acknowledgment of time asymmetry, the epistemological difference between past and future, and it would necessarily include a large subjective component, because everything about the piece but the content of the immediate present—thus everything that makes the present intelligible—can exist only in the mind of the participant as memory and projection. Such an analysis would proceed by maintaining a context for this present in the partial and conjectural way a participant does, not with the dogmatic certitude found in a score. It would be an analysis of the collaboration over time of sound and participant.

This approach is heretical in that it infiltrates analysis with ignorance. But presumably a needy restless ignorance of what is to be, emerging from a selective picture of what has been, is what participants want from music: certainly it is what they get. Surprise and disappointment and fulfillment would be basic terms in such an analysis.

The point of proposing this method here is to dismiss it, basing its dismissal on what I propose to be a basic drive underlying analysis. Processual analysis will never do because it renounces too much of the omniscience in detachment that is the analyst's central joy.

Music conditions its representations without determining them; certain representations of music—scores—make certain musical actualities—performances—possible, again without determining them completely; but the influence of representations on music extends beyond that one. The form that representations take shapes our perceptions of their originals; thus musical representations have a bearing on our general view of music, conditioning the music maker's sense of musical possibilities. And so it is important to be as clear as one can be about the image that each mode of representation projects.

Each medium in which we represent music projects an image of it adapted at least as much to the medium's own characteristics—those of verbalizing or picturing or gesturing—as to those of music itself, and each underrepresents whatever about music doesn't fit its own parameters. I conclude with a sampling of some of these images. They have in common a tendency to neutralize the qualities of temporal liquidity and perfusiveness characteristic of sound and so of music, and to replace them with something relatively circumscribed, locatable, and stabilized in time.

The gap is smallest with gestural representations, such as those of a conductor (remember Heraclitus: "only movement can know movement"). The music made visible through gesture is a muscular music situated somewhere between the visual and the kinesthetic, just as dance is: it acknowledges gravity, as sound does not, and the spatial separation of viewer and viewed to a degree that sound, and therefore music, does not; it is localized—in the body—as music, as sound generally is not. It lacks any reliable account of pitch. It tends to smooth over music's fine granularity through time: no sixty-fourth notes.

Furthest of all representations from music's native state are the graphic ones, such as scores and analytic diagrams, and it is tempting for that reason to see them as prototypical. This music is coldly detailed and inert; it seems to stare back at the reader like the figures in a wax museum, and only the rigorously trained imagination of a musician can perform the act of auditory seeing that will make it sing. For it is above all silent.

Music conveyed by words has a coarse, lumpy granularity, for music travels more lightly than does language, engorged as language is with syllables and meaning. Language represents the fine detail of music only occasionally and it is full of the distracting echoes that are started by the multiple significances of words. In any case, different levels of observation and judgment all tend to be subsumed in one flow, in a sequence independent of that in the original.

Each of these modes of representation is a semi-independent, complex, hybrid class of artifact that must be judged not just for what it says about music—and not just as gesture, or prose, or graphic design either. Meanwhile music's own precisions of pitch and rhythm lie apart in a domain of relentless emergence that represents a threat of vagueness and dissolution to that tropism of mind that seeks fixity and delimitation in the world, the tropism that has its fullest musical realization not in music itself but in music's metamorphoses into words and pictures.

Chapter Seven

INSTRUMENTALITIES

AN INTRIGUING ASPECT of musical instruments, considered simply as objects in themselves, is their unmusicality: their stolidly localized materiality is the antithesis of music's transient energy states diffusing through the air. And so instruments raise the same fundamental questions that were discussed in the previous chapter in connection with representations.

Perhaps their materiality helps to explain why instruments can't be discussed without raising extramusical issues, some of which will be taken up in this chapter. Besides embodying a conjunction of dense with rarefied—the density of their materials with the rarefaction of their musical product—instruments are a comment on the relation of performers' bodies to their living spaces: they raise questions about the interaction of skin-in with skin-out and about the control of the spaces around and between us.

Music is either sung or played, and performers on an instrument, a clarinet for example, reject the resources of the interior of the body used by singers in favor of an interaction with an object outside themselves. In either case, whether singing or playing the clarinet, the performers, by focusing and concentrating their breath, animate the space around them with what is literally an expression, a pushing outward of their energy. But in playing the clarinet performers hold their breath in their own hands where they can work on it and shape it out in the open, in full view of anyone who cares to watch.

Instruments are out there in the open, distributed through Field 1 like furniture, along with tables and beds and carpets. Furniture is, in one perspective, exactly what they are, and in a small way they participate in the grand human program of territorial appropriation. They diffuse the activity of making music through the other activities implied by mirrors and chairs and the rest of the furniture of domestic life and so mark its overlapping intersections with them. Though instruments are certainly easier to write about than is music itself because their physical stability submits so much better to scrutiny (a point made in Chapter 6 in connection with scores), their very familiarity creates another sort of problem for analysis: it is so hard truly to see a piano or a guitar and for the same reasons that make it hard to see a spoon or a telephone. Though in one perspective it is strange that so bizarre a device as a saxophone could ever be so taken for granted as to require de-familiarizing, the fact is that it is entirely assimilated to the everyday.

CHAPTER 2 described a generative-receptive loop associated with vocalizing, a closed circuit in which kinesthetic and auditory sensations confirm each other: the vocalizing self is transformed from the status of localized physical thing to that of circumambient energy state. What instruments do is to enlarge the loop, bringing outside matter and new manipulative skills into it and in so doing enlarging still further the performers' sense of their practical competence and consequence in the larger world. While the satisfactions of singing can be as great or greater than those of performing on an instrument, they are more purely self-centered.

Listeners may read the message of instrumental competence in the same way. Jane Goodall writes of a low-ranking chimpanzee she called Mike who was one of a group she observed over a long period at the Gombe Stream Reserve. Mike had an evident desire to improve his status in the group, but to do so he needed to compensate for his relatively small size. Lying around the compound were some empty four-gallon kerosene cans. Mike decided to hit them together as part of his power display, producing a powerful clangor, and this gave a considerable sonic boost to the respect with which he was treated by peers and rivals. A portable stereo carried down a city street makes a similar gesture.

Melodic instruments displace the innate starting point for sound making from the larynx, buried alive inside the body, to the outer illuminated world inhabited by the visible and tangible self. The point of inception for sound now assumes the form of an external object, a thing among things, accessible to fingers, eyes, lips, and sometimes feet too. But it retains a strong link with the body. Because so many instruments make use of semi-enclosed resonators, they form a special group among artifacts morphologically as well as functionally. Like containers of all kinds they mimic the body, with its semi-enclosed interior spaces, and the sounds they make emerge like the voice from hidden recesses. Again like the human body, these quasi-homunculi are not autonomous objects to the degree that, say, a crystal is, but assume the shapes they have down to the finest detail in relation to something outside themselves. An explanation for the form and composition of a fingerboard, like one for the human eye, lies outside structural considerations bearing solely on the article itself.

Each instrument fitted with a resonator takes possession of its space in a conquest by enclosure—just as the body does—and often musicians take possession of the instruments themselves through acts of envelopment, wrapping their hands around them, their arms too, or, in the case of a cello for example, much of the body. Musicians and listeners are themselves typically enfolded. A hall meant for the performance of music is like the walk-in, wrap-around resonator of some giant lute.

This anthropomorphic aspect of many instruments is the focus of much of their symbolic significance. Symbolism is not the subject of this essay, but its workings can be suggested by recalling the Russian proverb that states that "a wife is not an instrument you can hang on the wall when you're tired playing on it." This invites the speculation that an instrument may sometimes be a kind of wife whose special virtue is that she *can* be hung on the wall when you have had enough of her. Bluesman B. B. King's guitar was named Lucille, and before Lucille it was Betsy for twenty years. Like the human body, the body of an instrument is a fixity that is all about potential movement, in this case the movement of sound waves; only—and this constitutes a recommendation for anyone who needs a surrogate lover who is no more than an extension of him- or herself—the movements of an instrument are purely reactive. It is responsive and nothing but responsive (this statement needs qualification in the case of some electronic instruments). Many instruments offer the special advantage in a lover of portability.

We can't wait to get our hands on things, as the expression

goes—hands are even involved in speech much of the time. Singers sometimes don't seem to know what to do with their hands: their activity is concentrated so intensely on the body's interior that hands, having overwhelmingly to do with what is skin-out, can feel left over, so that the singer may be grateful for a microphone or handkerchief to hold on to. Hands are the means of our cleverest interventions in our surroundings, central to the activities of detaching things from their native settings and carrying them around. They are so integral to the human way of doing things that the expression "empty handed" carries with it connotations of inadequacy. Fingers carry intervention a degree further in the direction of fine detail, and a rough parallel exists between the progression in degree of temporal refinement from rhythm to pitch in music, and the progression from the trunk of the body out through arms and hands and finally fingers as the instrumentalist's means of controlling these musical dimensions.

The word "digit" can mean number as well as finger—fingers were presumably in on the beginnings both of counting and of stabilizing pitches on aerophones and chordophones. This points up a parallel between the domains of number and music: both stable pitches and numbers are discrete positions along a continuum. Clutching is a global sort of activity compared to the finely discriminating analytical work performed by fingers.

With all but the aerophones, hands detach music from the act (though almost never from the rhythm) of breathing. Some percussion instruments have almost nothing to do with displaced vocalism but instead start out with and celebrate the interaction of the body's surface, primarily through the agency of the hands, with its surroundings. Actually instruments are situated at the intersection of two directionally opposed tropisms, one of them being the urge to push or reach out from the body's interior, the other the urge to pull things in from the outside and establish them within the body's sphere of influence. Externalizing the threshold where sound begins necessarily means embodying it in new thresholds of bronze, clay, bamboo, bone, hair, and so on appropriated from our surroundings. Giving a voice to metals and woods means giving life and movement to the inanimate, converting its stillness to resiliency.

The fact that these objects, inanimate in themselves, exist for the purpose of being animated gives them another significance. Different times converge in them. The hands of an instrument maker achieved this fixed result and achieved it at some particular time in the past which is brought up into the present with the survival of his handiwork. In performance, this result responds to the hands of a performer who may be actualizing a program thought through by a musician—working at his own rate of speed—from some quite different period in the past. All of this movement is implied in the still body of the instrument. Instruments are the most fixed and tangible component in the least fixed and tangible of the arts. We can grip instruments and possess them as we can't music, or time itself, because they are firmly embedded in Field 1. Sometimes more of the effort that goes into their making is directed at the connoisseur of fine visual objects than at the lover of music. Instruments can serve a function parallel to one of the functions of representations discussed in Chapter 6: they are visible and tangible symbols of our power over the special power that sound has over us—more radically still, over the very passage of time itself.

LIKE KEROSENE cans clashed together, sounding musical instruments add something fresh and challenging to the contents of the world. Unlike kerosene cans, instruments, with their frets and keys and mouthpieces, are fashioned in detail to receive our initiatives: they are outside us without being alien to us. They can be thought of as related to what the psychoanalytical theorist D. W. Winnicott called "transitional objects," childhood articles such as blankets or stuffed toys that have a constructively ambiguous status between the small child's self and the child's emergent sense of otherness. They help the child bridge the gap between a stage of assumed omnipotence (sustained in fact by total dependency) and the mature phase in which self and other are discriminated. They can do so because they are at once external to the body, part of the outside world, and at the same time as responsive to the child's will as though they were extensions of the body. Perhaps we seldom do completely make the transition to autonomy, some of us experiencing more difficulty with it than others do. Perhaps the provisional solution represented by transitional objects survives early childhood along with the problem of establishing a reciprocal relationship with the outside world that it was meant to deal with, attaching itself to new objects such as pipes, chewing gum, pet animals—and musical instruments.

Considered as "transitional objects," instruments participate in what Winnicott called the "third area, that of play, which expands into creative living and into the whole cultural life of man. This third area [contrasts] with inner or personal psychic reality and with the actual world in which the individual lives, which can be objectively perceived. I have located this important area of *experience* in the potential space between the individual and the environment. . . . "

Musical instruments join artifacts of all sorts in this area: screwdrivers, shotguns, telescopes, masks—all the armamentarium of indirection—and even such activities as language, ritual,

114

play, and art itself. Winnicott's "third area" is in the old and honorable philosophical tradition that takes mediacy to be the principal key to human nature and sees much of what is distinctively human as an array of interpolations—some of them individual, some collective—between us and the surrounding world. The space so fitted out can function either as a buffer zone to keep the outside at a safe distance (insofar as it contains things like walls and clothing) or as a staging area for focusing an attack on it (tools of all kinds). The entire zone with all its contents is the precipitate of thought, of action in Field 2. Musical instruments, along with instruments and tools generally, are transitional in a way that goes beyond the developmental sense intended by Winnicott and applied by him to security blankets and cuddly toys. They are transitional in a more assured and active way, a more developmentally evolved way, in that their existence implies full acknowledgment of a separate environment and an intention of adding to it or otherwise making a difference in it.

TESTING THE concept "transitional object" for its applicability to musical instruments focuses on the relationship between instrument and performer. Shifting to the interaction between performer and listener suggests another concept, that of the mask. Masks conceal, but they can do more: a ritual or theatrical mask is an interpolation that depersonalizes, or rather repersonalizes, the actor (persona = mask), for the surface of the mask can be worked up into a stylized and grandly expressive new surface. Similarly, an instrument replaces the performer's own sonic face, the voice, with a culturally approved impersonal sound used only for making music.

True, the technique of a trained singer takes the natural voice some distance in that same direction. But a given instrument necessarily imposes a greater degree of timbral standardization on its performers than is found among singers—even among a special class of singers, such as mezzo-sopranos. Collectively, instruments broaden the timbral options, but do so in tight clusters: "ophicleide," "banjo," and so forth. A piano key depressed with a certain velocity will produce the same sound no matter who so depresses it. The tone produced by a dozen different pianists will be more nearly uniform than the sounds of their voices, and very likely more uniformly pleasing: musical ability has a different distribution pattern throughout the population than does vocal quality. With respect to native tone, all pianists start out even. By minimizing tone as a consideration bearing on comparisons among artists, instruments have the effect of concentrating attention on more essentially musical considerations.

Probably the very existence of the folklore that says that the character of various instruments matches the personalities of their performers (the high-strung violinist, the bluff, hearty trombone player) is more informative than its content. But a better model than the mask for this construal of the instrument in its relationship to the performer would be the ventriloquist's dummy. For here the maneuver is not simply one of concealment and transformation but involves splitting the performer's personality and displacing part of it onto an alter ego that acts as a foil, not a clone. This model leaves room for possible bluff, hearty violinists and high-strung trombone players.

With masks and ventriloquists' dummies—and musical instruments—performers exercise control over the surface they present to a perceiver, control not so different from that exercised by the wearer of clothes, which are after all a kind of all-but-the-face mask. In all these cases there is a retreat from intimacy with viewers and listeners, in the case of music from the intimacy of vocal performance (singer Mary Mayo once said in an interview that "whether I like it or not, when I stand there singing I'm naked"). Something similar takes place in moving from the spoken to the written word. A retreat from intimacy may be exactly what is sought on both sides, but at least some of the time the interpolation of a new surface has another consequence, that of facilitating an opening out from the personal onto something more encompassing. A particular voice, a particular face always bring with them some of the atmosphere of ordinary mortality, a particular life situation and life history, and depersonalization liberates expressivity from all such restrictive associations. Being free of words, instrumental performance is also independent of the personal point of view from which remarks are necessarily offered.

Opera shows how this potential can be used. The opera orchestra doesn't just frame and pace the proceedings, it almost always knows best, in contrast to the frequently deluded personas on stage. Without a particular human identity and point of view, it provides a polyphonically disinterested commentary on events (inevitably one thinks of the impersonally interlocutory role of the chorus in the ancient Greek theater). Instruments can achieve a kind of directness impossible for the voice, a mediated immediacy. The latter-day technology of instrument building brings about a regression to a purer primitive voice, the voice as it was before words, before individuation—it helps the effect that this voice issues from beneath the level of the stage—enabling composer and audience to conspire at omniscience. As with the archetype of the holy fool, the trade-off for omniscience is a renunciation of articulacy.

BEFORE CONCLUDING, something should be said about the most obvious and straightforward role played by instruments.

In relation to music itself they act as energy transformers—this is the kind of thing tools generally are about—enriching the resources available to music making. The performer's energy is transformed timbrally, registrally, dynamically—some instruments convert the essentially monophonic resources of the performer into polyphony. This extended spectrum is further enriched when instruments are combined in mixed groupings: gamelan and string quartet are examples of standardized composite instruments. Since instrumental sounds have so few uses outside of music, they help to bracket music (to a degree the voice cannot) as a territory apart. And once musical sound is conceived as a territory, the invention and cultivation of instruments can be understood as the result of a drive for territorial conquest. The modern European history of instruments realizes a program of sonic imperialism crudely analogous to, and synchronous with, the geopolitical one.

Another possible parallel involves European cultural history. The period of instrumental imperialism began in the fifteenth century and reached its climax in the decades around 1610, and this coincided with a fundamental change in broad outlook in the society as a whole. This had many aspects, but a new concern with theatricality is one that it suits my present purposes to stress, along with one other, the increasing authority of the scientific outlook with its program of theory building. This pairing of "theory" with "theater" is not casual, because both words derive from the Greek root *theōrein*, meaning "to see," and both point to a taste for the vicarious, for indirect participation that derives from aspirations to a kind of ideal mastery that can only be achieved in detachment.

The seventeenth century has been called the great age of theater. In the theater a narrative unfolds on a stage, a space removed from the spectator who maintains a detached overview of the proceedings. In science, performances called experiments, typically staged in laboratories, are expected to lead to synoptic, masterful overviews called theorems or laws. And the success of the new science was dependent on the emergence of a new class of instruments for enhancing vision and bringing a new degree of precision to measurement: telescopes and microscopes, barometers and thermometers.

There is no claim here that all instrumental performance originates in aspirations to a detached mastery of the world. In fact, the view taken of the role of instruments in east and southeast Asia is something like the reverse of this, for there it is performers who are seen as the instruments of forces outside themselves, and the instruments themselves as being, in some cases, means by which the gods act on mortal performers, exacting their duties from them. Nevertheless it does seem suggestive that the first great age of purely instrumental music in Europe should have come along at the same time as two great cultural movements expressing a parallel interest in mastery in detachment, the scientific revolution and the resurgence of theater. In the cases both of music and of science, detachment involved the use of mechanical aids: scientific instruments helped discover a world, musical instruments to build one.

Conclusion

THIS BOOK has surveyed the involvement and participation of human activities involving sound, principally speech and music, in three heuristic fields that might be characterized briefly as the fields of body, mind, and spirit.

From the point of view of the physical production of sound, the site of the divide between Fields 1 and 2 is the separation between throat and mouth, the points of origin of, respectively, vocal tone and oral phonation, and thus of inarticulate cries and speech. The system formed by throat and mouth can be thought of as the physiological point of reference for a central and defining duality in human affairs, one that, as was suggested in Chapter 3, lies behind various of the oppositions conventionally used in characterizing human nature, such as that of body and mind or of feeling and thought. The throat/mouth pairing was proposed as an elaboration of a more basic expressive mechanism outlined in Chapter 2, one not limited to humans, in which the opposition of exhaled air and the tightened vocal folds, issuing in growls and moans and shrieks, in inarticulate vocal sound generally, is used to enact the state of the relationship between self and other.

The cohabitation of Fields 1 and 2 need not be uneasy. But the differences between what they contain and the differences between their ruling topologies are great. Field 1 is under the sign of necessity, dictated by the body's mereness and mortality, its compact localization in the physical world of distances and resistances. By comparison, Field 2 offers a new degree of freedom. It is placeless, utopian in the root sense of that term, in that thought, which is the form that action takes in this field, breaks with the here and now—in fact, play is thought's hard necessity: presumably thought's capacity for playing with the possibilities implied but not realized in the actual was its contribution to the survival and prosperity of the thinking animal. In its ability to deal with everything from the minute particulars to the synoptic overview, thinking has the perspectival adaptability of a zoom lens; it operates in the past, the future, and the elsewhere; it has the freedom to originate and the freedom to erase; Field 2 is the native habitat of the notion of free will.

Freedom in Field 2 can also be a vertiginous freedom from the feeling of solid earth under foot, of location relative to the features of the surrounding terrain that is normally taken for granted in Field 1. Whenever it is without fixed coordinates, without rules and limits, whether received or imposed, Field 2 is a chaos, and thought is free then to be painfully alienated from the situation of the body and divided against itself. But the emancipation of Field 2 from Field 1 could never in any case be complete, since mind is tethered to body—it might be thought of as the body's attenuated dilation—and thought's accountability must ultimately be to the body (including the collective body: family, tribe, species) and its fate.

I have argued in this book for a large evolutionary role for sound in the ballooning out of Field 2 in humans (and so indirectly a large share of the responsibility for the stresses within Field 2 and for those between 2 and 1). Relatively detached from the look and the location of things in Field 1, sound makes available to communication a potential for utopian play that the human discovery of oral phonation released in speech, and that the invention of pitch classes and rhythms released in music.

Sound shaped into music is perhaps the most direct way into Field 3, and Field 3 is a way out of 1 and 2 and the strains within and between them. Field 3 forgives mereness and mortality. Action here turns back on itself and converges on stasis. When Field 3 is fully realized, there can be no friction between part and part, part and whole—there are no parts, and so no particulars, and no partiality. There is no possible disorientation, for there is only one possible orientation, and that is to be one with the whole.

APPENDIX

Purcell's setting of the first two lines of Dryden's "Music for a while," illustrating its musical distortion and dismemberment of the text. From Orpheus Britannicus, 3d ed. (London, 1721; reprint, Ridgewood, N.J.: Gregg Press, 1965), vol. 2.

beats	1	2	3	4	1	2	3	4
PURCELL	Mu_____sick,				Mu_____sick for a			
DRYDEN	Musick for a while							

	1	2	3	4	1	2	3	4
PURCELL	while,	Shall all your Cares be–guile;			shall all			all,
DRYDEN		Shall your cares beguile						

	1	2	3	4	1	2	3	4	1
PURCELL	all,	shall all,		all, all		shall all your Cares be–guile;			
DRYDEN									

—dain—ing to be pleas'd, till *A—lec—to* free the Dead, till *A—lec—to* free the Dead, from

their E—ter— — — —nal, E—ter— — — — — nal Band;

till the *Snakes* drop, drop, drop, drop, drop, drop, drop, drop, drop from her Head; and the

Whip, and the Whip from out her Hand; Musick, Musick for a while shall

all your cares beguile; shall all, all, all, all, all, all, all, shall all your cares be——

—guile; all, all, all, all, all, all, all, all, shall all, your cares be—guile.

Notes

I received some encouragement for my sketch of the relations between action in Fields 1 and 2 from Mark Johnson, *The Body in the Mind: The Bodily Basis of Meaning, Imagination, and Reason* (Chicago, 1987), where he shows how the mechanical constraints on physical action exert a force on the stories we tell.

"The Infinite Sphere: Comments on the History of a Metaphor" by Karsten Harries (*Journal of the History of Philosophy* 13 [1975]) details the historical transference of the image of a sphere whose center is everywhere and its periphery nowhere from God to the universe.

CHAPTER ONE / SOUND

The quotation from Donald A. Ramsdell is from his chapter, "The Psychology of the Hard-of-Hearing and the Deafened Adult," in *Hearing and Deafness,* ed. Halowell Davis (New York, 1947), p. 396. The quotation from Nietzsche is no. 250 in his *Gedanken über Moral (Musarionausgabe* 10, P. 218). Anthony Jackson's comment about ritual specialists comes from his "Sound and Ritual," *Man* 3 (1968): 296.

"Visual and Auditory Perception: An Essay of Comparison" by Bela Julesz and Ira J. Hirsh offers a thorough review of the subject from the point of view of experimental psychology. It is found in Edward E. David and Peter B. Denes, eds., *Human Communication: A Unified View* (New York, 1972), 283–340.

Important influences on my own thinking at an early stage were Erwin Straus, *Phenomenological Psychology,* trans. Erling Eng (New York, 1966), and Helmuth Plessner, "Zur Anthropologie der Musik," in *Jahrbuch für Aesthetik und Kunstwissenschaft* (1953). "The Nobility of Sight: A Study in the Phenomenology of the Senses" by Hans Jonas is another revealing study by a philosopher. It is found in his *Phenomenon of Life: Toward a Philosophical Biology* (New York, 1966). There is a detailed and valuable phenomenological account of sound in Walter J. Ong, *The Presence of the Word: Some Prolegomena for Cultural and Religious History* (1967; Minneapolis, 1981). Don Ihde carries forward the tradition of Husserl in *Listening and Voice: A Phenomenology of Sound* (Athens, Ohio, 1976). R. Murray Schafer's book *The Tuning of the World* (New York, 1977) contains a valuable anthology of sound lore distributed through its argument.

In Africa, " 'Hearing' in the wider sense is a concept that includes hearing, smell and taste, so that perception is thought of in two main groups: vision and contact" according to Janheinz Jahn in *Muntu: Outline of the New African Culture* (New York, 1961), 122. This view gets a kind of confirmation from physiology: the same stretch-activated gating mechanism controls both touch and hearing (see Frederick Sachs, "The Intimate Sense: Understanding the Mechanics of Touch," in *The Sciences* 28, no. 1 [1988]). Gilbert Rouget has some vivid paragraphs on the physical interconnection of listener and sound source in *Music and Trance: A Theory of the Relations between Music and Possession,* trans. Brunhilde Biebuyck (Chicago, 1985), 119–21, and William S. Condon and Louis W. Sander have shown that listening to speech is physically fine tuned before we understand it: "Synchrony Demonstrated between Movements of the Neonate and Adult Speech," *Child Development*, no. 45 (1974): 456–62. For a searching exploration of the involvement of sound in the whole life of a people, see Steven Feld, *Sound and Sentiment: Birds, Weeping, Poetics, and Song in Kaluli Expression* (Philadelphia, 1982).

Two studies of silence are Max Picard, *The World of Silence*, trans. Stanley Godman (London, n.d.), and Bernard P. Danenhauer, *Silence: The Phenomenon and Its Ontological Significance* (Bloomington, Ind., 1980).

CHAPTER TWO / VOICE

Toni Morrison's novel is *The Bluest Eyes* (1970; New York, 1972), and the passage quoted is from p. 16. Herbert Spencer's remarks are taken from his essay "The Origin and Function of Music," for which my source was his *Literary Style and Music* (London, 1950). Alan Lomax's observations about vocal tension are found in *Folk Song Style and Culture* (Washington, D.C., 1968), 194–96. My information about bird song comes from W. H. Thorpe, *Bird Song: The Biology of Vocal Communication and Expression in Birds* (Cambridge, 1961). Elias Canetti describes the Kraus lecture in Canetti, *The Torch in My Ear*, trans. Joachim Neugroschel (New York, 1982), 70–71.

Voices, in particular the voices of singers, can be regarded as aesthetic objects in themselves, rather than as the means to further communicative ends. This seems to be the point of view of the author of the following critical catalog of voice types, written at the time and in the place of origin of the *bel canto:* "Voce sonora, e perfetta; Voce flebile; Voce di petto, e di testa; Voce ineguale, grassa, e crescente; Voce che cala; Voce debole, cruda, & aspra; Voce mistica di più registri; Voce bovina, nascina, capretina, e raganella; Voce ottusa, & in gola; Voce instabile, che non stà ne in spatio, ne in riga; e finalmente Voce falsa, e male organizzata, . . . " ("The sonorous and perfect voice; the plaintive voice; the voice from the chest and head; the uneven, fleshy, and swelling voice; the voice that dies away; the weak, raw, and harsh voice; the mystical voice of different registers; the cowlike, [asinine?], goatlike, and froglike voice; the dull, throat-produced voice; the unstable voice, fixed neither in space nor on the staff; and finally, the false and badly-placed voice . . . "). From Angelo Berardi, *Miscellanea Musicale* (Bologna, 1689), 43.

A varied collection of essays on "voice," mostly in the literary sense, is Norman F. Cantor and Nathalia King, eds., *Voice*, vol. 3 of *Notebooks in Cultural Analysis* (Durham, N.C., 1986).

CHAPTER THREE / WORDS

Robert Frost's characterization of the sentence is found in a letter to John Bartlett, February 22, 1914, in *Selected Letters of Robert Frost*, ed. Lawrence Thompson (New York, 1964), 110. Hockett discusses design features of communications systems in C. F. Hockett, "The Origin of Speech," *Scientific American* 203 (1960): 10–11. Collins's observations have been given in conversations and class lectures. Emily Dickinson's letter to Thomas Wentworth Higginson is quoted in Thomas H. Johnson, *Emily Dickinson: An Interpretive Biography* (Cambridge, Mass., 1955), 51–52.

Philip Lieberman's "source-filter" theory is relevant to my discussion of speech production, as is much else in his authoritative book, *The Biology and Evolution of Language* (Cambridge, 1984).

To my knowledge, the closest approach until now to my attempt to establish a connection between the character of vocal sound and that of thought is found in the work of two contemporary philosophers, P. F. Strawson and Daniel C. Dennett. Strawson makes sound the substance of a hypothetical "no-space world" in *Individuals* (London, 1959), and Dennett uses "voice" as a model in his inquiry into "the ontological status of mind," because it has a status analogous to that of mind in standing apart from "the referential domain of the physical sciences"—see his *Content and Consciousness* (New York, 1969), chapter 1, esp. 8–18.

CHAPTER FOUR / WORDS AND MUSIC

George List's remarks on Hopi and Australian aboriginal song will be found in two of his articles: "Hopi Melodic Concepts," *Journal of the American Musicological Society* 38 (Spring 1985): 143–52, and "The Boundaries of Speech and Song," *Ethnomusicology* 7 (1963).

The Sound Shape of Language by Roman Jakobson and Linda R. Waugh (Bloomington, Ind., 1979) is full of observations relevant to this chapter, including the reference I quote to the term "vyañjana."

Chazel's aphorism was taken from *The Viking Book of Aphorisms*, ed. W. H. Auden and Louis Kronenberger (Harmondsworth, 1981), 15. Edward T. Cone's book is *The Composer's Voice* (Berkeley, 1974).

Philip Lieberman's article, "On the Evolution of Human Syntactic Ability," *Journal of Human Evolution* 14 (1985): 657–68, discusses the parallel evolution of brain and supralaryngeal articulatory capacity in support of the capability for speech. I have depended on Howard Gardner's review of what can be learned from brain-damaged patients about the localization of musical ability in the brain: *Art, Mind, and Brain* (New York, 1982), 327–30. Psychoanalytic views of the roots of music making are surveyed in Pinchas Noy, "The Psychodynamic Meaning of Music," *Journal of Music Therapy* 3, no. 4 (1966) and ibid. 4, nos. 1–4 (1967).

A good picture of recent work in the semiotics of music will be found in "Basic Concepts of Studies in Musical Signification: A Report on a New International Research Project in Semiotics of Music," compiled by Eero Tarasti (in *The Semiotic Web, '86: An International Yearbook*, ed. Thomas A. Sebeok and Jean Umiker-Sebeok [Berlin, 1987]). For a philosopher's perspective, see Peter Kivy, *Sound and Semblance: Reflections on Musical Representation* (Princeton, 1984).

My formulation of the contrasting orientations associated with speech and music was influenced by a suggestion of Joseph E. Bogen's growing out of his research into the hemispheric lateralization of the brain: "Each hemisphere represents the other and the world in complementary mappings: the left mapping the self as a subset of the world and the right mapping the world as a subset of the self." From "Hemispheric Specificity, Complementarity, and Self-Referential Mappings," in *Program and Abstracts*, Society for Neuroscience Third Annual Meeting, 1973.

Victor Zuckerkandl held a view of music in relation to speech that I judge to be similar to mine, based on passages such as the following: "People sing in order to make sure, through direct experience, of their existence in a layer of reality different from the one in which they encounter each other and things as speakers, as facing one another and separate from one another—in order to be aware of their existence on a plane where distinction and separation of man and man, man and thing, thing and thing give way to unity, to authentic togetherness" (*Man the Musician: Sound and Symbol*, trans. Norbert Guterman, vol. 2, Bollingen Series 44, no. 2 [Princeton, 1973], 42).

CHAPTER FIVE / WORDS IN MUSIC

Figaro says "Aujourd'hui ce qui ne vaut pas la peine d'être dit, on le chante" in Beaumarchais's *Barbier de Seville*, act 1, scene 2. Joseph Addison's comment comes from *The Spectator* 18 (March 21, 1711). Goethe's remark is quoted by Luigi Ronga in *The Meeting of Poetry and Music* (New York, 1956), 82, and A. H. Fox Strangway includes his trenchant observation in "A Song Translator's Notes," *Monthly Musical Record* 77, no. 887 (June 1947): 128.

Oedipus is found in volume 13, ed. Maximillian E. Novak, of *The Works of John Dryden*, ed. Alan Roper (Berkeley, 1984). "Music for a while" occurs in the middle of an extended musical masque in act 3, scene 1, and is found on page 166 of this edition. Schoenberg's comments occur in "The Relationship to the Text," in his *Style and Idea*, ed. Leonard Stein, trans. Leo Balck (London, 1975), 141–45. Mendelssohn's words are found in *Letters of Felix Mendelssohn Bartholdy from 1833 to 1847*, ed. Paul Mendelssohn Bartholdy and Carl Mendelssohn Bartholdy, trans. Lady Wallace [*sic*] (Philadelphia, 1864).

Section 6 of Nietzsche's *Birth of Tragedy*, trans. Walter Kaufman (New York, 1967), gives his views on the dependence of lyric verse on music. Susanne K. Langer states her position that music tends to be the dominant partner in song in *Feeling and Form* (New York, 1953), 152, and in "The Principle of Assimilation," *The Score*, no. 24 (November 1958): 42–53.

A history of the relations between texts and their musical settings in Europe is James Anderson Winn's *Unsuspected Eloquence* (New Haven, 1981).

Mark W. Booth summarizes the special characteristics of words for music in *The Experience of Songs* (New Haven, 1981), 7–9, 24.

CHAPTER SIX / WORDS ON MUSIC

The statement by Roland Barthes is taken from "The Grain of the Voice," in *The Responsibility of Forms*, trans. Richard Howard (New York, 1985), 267.

Chéret's lithograph is reproduced in Eugen Weber, *France: Fin de Siècle* (Cambridge, Mass., 1986), 169. A reproduction of the drawing by Stravinsky is in Igor Stravinsky and Robert Craft, *Conversations with Igor Stravinsky* (New York, 1959), 120.

The quotation from Elaine Scarry is taken from her *Body in Pain: The Making and Unmaking of the World* (New York, 1985), 4. Cynthia Ozick gives the quotation from Bialik in "Sholem Aleichem's Revolution," *The New Yorker*, 28 March 1988, 102. Kohut and Levarie's article, "On the Enjoyment of Music," appeared in *Psychoanalytic Quarterly* 19 (1950): 64–87.

The quotation from Freud will be found in "The Moses of Michelangelo," in *Collected Papers of Sigmund Freud*, vol. 4 (New York, 1959), 257. *Talk: If I Am a Musical Thinker* (Barrytown, N.Y., 1985) contains the passage by Benjamin Boretz. Heraclitus is quoted from *Herakleitos and Diogenes*, trans. Guy Davenport (San Francisco, 1981), 18.

Charles Seeger, in his *Studies in Musicology 1935–1975* (Berkeley, 1977), calls the relationship between music and its descriptions and analyses "the musicological juncture," though "disjuncture" would fit his characterization of it better. As far as I am aware, his is the solidest discussion of this point in the literature to date. In part a critique of Seeger is Steven Feld, "Communication, Music, and Speech about Music," in *1984 Yearbook for Traditional Music*, ed. Adelaida Reyes Schramm (International Council for Traditional Music), 1–18. Feld makes a claim for "the primacy of the social, interactive, intersubjective" aspect of participation in music and stresses the role of metaphor in verbalizing the experience.

Henri Bergson's views on the dependence of scrutiny on fixity have had a strong influence on my own. Here is a representative passage from *An Introduction to Metaphysics*, trans. T. E. Hulme (New York, 1912), 65–66: "Our mind, which seeks for solid points of support, has for its main function in the ordinary course of life that of representing *states* and *things. . . .* It starts from the immobile and only conceives and expresses movement as a function of immobility."

The subject of this chapter overlaps with the orality/literacy crux, too large a topic to be taken up here; for an overview see Walter J. Ong, *Orality and Literacy: The Technologizing of the Word* (New York, 1982). Leo Treitler has dealt with it extensively for music; see, for example, his "Reading and Singing: On the Genesis of Occidental Music-Writing," in *Early Music History* 4 (1984): 135–208.

Gilbert Rouget documents the link between music and altered states of consciousness in *Music and Trance* cited in Chapter 1.

The literary critic Stanley Fish once proposed a processual approach to the analysis of literature: "The basis of the method is a consideration of the *temporal* flow of the reading experience, and it is assumed that the reader responds in terms of that flow and not to the whole utterance. That is, in an utterance of any length, there is a point at which the reader has taken in only the first word, and then the second, and then the third, and so on, and the report of what happens to the reader is always a report of what has happened *to that point.* (The report includes the reader's set toward future experiences, but not those experiences)" ("Literature in the Reader: Affective Stylistics," an essay of 1970 reprinted in his *Is There a Text in This Class?* [Cambridge, Mass., 1980], 27). Without knowledge of Fish's essay I once before brought up the possibility of "a kind of calculus of musical process": "Music and the Biology of Time," *Perspectives of New Music* 11, no. 1 (1972): 248. The model of the perception of music developed in Leonard B. Meyer's classic study *Emotion and Meaning in Music* (Chicago, 1956) is relevant to this topic.

Patricia Carpenter's richly thoughtful article "The Musical Object" (*Current Musicology* 5 [1967]) reviews the literature on time in music and points to degrees of stylization toward objectness as a central variable in the history of European music.

CHAPTER SEVEN / INSTRUMENTALITIES

The story of Mike comes from Jane Goodall's *In the Shadow of Man* (Boston, 1971), 112–14.

D. W. Winnicott's views on transitional objects and the third area will be found in his *Playing and Reality* (New York, 1971). The passage I have quoted is on pp. 103–4.

Mary Mayo is quoted by Whitney Balliett in *The New Yorker*, 27 February 1978.

Curt Sachs, *The History of Musical Instruments* (New York, 1940), contains many observations about the symbolic import of instruments.

Rodney Needham has noted a connection between percussion instruments and another sort of transition, the shaman's entering into communication with the supernatural world: "Percussion and Transition," *Man* 2 (1967): 606–14.

The relationship between instruments and personality is the subject of Chapter 13 in John Booth Davies's *Psychology of Music* (Stanford, 1978).

The period from the fifteenth through the seventeenth centuries in the history of musical instruments is covered in Chapters 15 and 16 in Sachs, *History of Musical Instruments*, cited above. H. R. Trevor-Roper's *Crisis of the Seventeenth Century* (New York, 1968) gives a vivid picture of the age. The importance of scientific instruments to scientific activity at the time is discussed in Derek de Solla Price, *Science Since Babylon*, enl. ed. (New Haven, 1975), 49, and elsewhere.

My information about the role of musical instruments in east and southeast Asia was contained in a personal communication from Tilman Seebass.

Index